MAXZYNE *meets*
the
MANNEQUINS

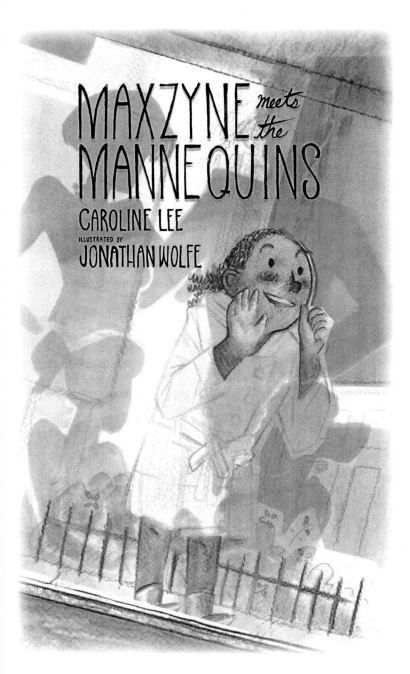

MAXZYNE meets the MANNEQUINS

CAROLINE LEE

ILLUSTRATED BY
JONATHAN WOLFE

Pendant Press, LLC.
Chicago, IL

Pendant Press, LLC.

Summary: When a lonely 10-year-old sneaks out of her Chicago high-rise to swim alone, she encounters a family of vintage mannequins from a nearby department store who will lose their heads unless she can save them, but the rescue mission is in jeopardy until she stops being sidetracked by her own imagination and desires.

Key words: fiction, Chicago, adventure, mannequins, friendship, generosity, homelessness, visual merchandising, art

ISBN 978-0-9906617-0-2
LCCN: 2015932307

Cover art and interior illustrations by Jonathan Wolfe, ©2012
Typeset by Sophie Chi

Printed in the United States of America

For Rebecca

Contents

1

Polly

"I WISH I COULD PLAY with you!" Maxzyne breathes to the colorful poodle mannequin on the other side of the glass. The puff of warm air leaves a tiny burst of fog on the window of the old department store. She admires the large Easter egg the dog holds between two paws. "I'd sure have fun in a place that believes in polka-dot poodles. I wish you were real." She quickly traces a heart on the glass before the fog disappears.

"Maxzyne! Did you hear me?"

Maxzyne imagines the poodle rushing to the window, barking excitedly. In her mind, she sees the dog roll the egg her way, inviting her to play. The delightful fantasy vanishes as Mother hurries over, shopping bags in hand. She frowns, sidestepping a puddle of cappuccino that stains the sidewalk. A light gust of wind swirls the hem of her stylish cashmere sweater coat and tugs at the crackling, white tissue paper in the bags she carries. Mother shivers and sighs with impatience. She raises dark sunglasses that make her look like an owl and peers at the window display.

"What is it this time? If there's a distraction to be found, you'll find it. So what's got your head in the clouds now?"

"That poodle. Look! He's helping the blonde girl hide the eggs by the chair over there. See?"

Mother glances at the old-fashioned Easter scene. A smartly dressed couple exchanges Easter baskets. Nearby, kneeling beside a Chippendale chair, their daughter hides eggs with the poodle. With a quick nod, Mother pulls the sunglasses back down over her eyes. "Very nice. But we don't have time for this right now, do we?" She playfully tugs one of Maxzyne's braids where a strand of hair has escaped. "Your father expects our bags to be packed when he gets home tonight," she reminds her daughter. "We have to be at the airport early tomorrow." Glancing at the window again, she pauses. "Those mannequins are different, aren't they? Hmm. They must be quite old. I wonder where they've been hiding all these decades."

Maxzyne sighs, trailing her finger across the glass. She stops in front of the blonde girl mannequin. She admires her smocked yellow-and-white dress trimmed with daisies and the wide matching ribbon that pulls her hair into a tight ponytail. Behind the girl, her mannequin parents pretend to cover their eyes.

"Aw! Aren't they cute?" Maxzyne gushes. "I bet her poodle even talks—listen!" Maxzyne holds her ear to the window, grinning. "He just told me he knows where all the Millennium Park eggs are hidden!"

"I know where this is going, young lady. Before your imagination runs wild, as it usually does—no! There will not be a puppy in your Easter basket, nor a cell phone! You're just lucky we're going to the beach and getting away from this awful weather." Mother shivers again. She shifts her bags to one hand and pulls her shawl collar higher on her neck.

"But we'll miss the big Easter egg hunt in the park! Oh, please, can't we stay here for once? I could sleep over with Erika and Gayle. They're going. It's not fair."

"Give up our spring beach week? Our plans are made!" She raises her sunglasses to look directly at Maxzyne. "And no sleepovers 'til you're thirteen. You know the rules." Looking down the sidewalk in the direction of home, Mother turns to leave.

"But it's so boring when it's just us. Dad's always working. Even on vacation he's on the phone or his computer with—"

Someone pushes between them, interrupting Maxzyne's plea. Maxzyne glances at the tall, black woman trailing a beat-up suitcase and clutching a dingy, overstuffed shopping bag. The hood of her long, red cape shadows her eyes. *It gives her an air of mystery,* Maxzyne thinks. The young girl grows more fascinated when the woman smiles and begins talking to the mannequin girl beside the poodle in the window.

"Yoo hoo! Missy! Look at those pretty daisies you're showing today. Mighty fine, mighty fine."

Immediately, Mother's nose begins to twitch. Her

lips purse tightly in annoyance. She grabs her daughter by the coat collar and begins to back away. But before Mother can get far enough, the homeless woman pulls a small painting from her bag. She pushes it into Maxzyne's hand. Mother strides off, dragging her daughter along.

"See what I mean?" Mother's eyes flash. "Really, Maxzyne! Your silly daydreaming attracts all sorts, doesn't it? Now come on!" She takes her daughter by the hand.

With her free hand, Maxzyne raises the rough paper to eye level and smiles. Awesome! Swirls of pastel polka-dots decorate a white poodle, just like the one in Crowne's Emporium window. Had the stranger read her mind? She turns, hoping to see the stranger. Perhaps there is still time to thank her.

But Mother simply walks faster until a muffled ringtone claims her attention. Releasing Maxzyne's hand, she reaches inside her oversized purse. "It's your father. He said he'd call about now." She pulls out a turquoise cell phone. "Hello, there . . ."

In a flash, Maxzyne is off. Her blue, high-top sneakers sprint down the sidewalk, and her braids bounce. *Now where'd that lady go?* she wonders, looking up and down the street. *She can't be far, right?* To her left, there is a flash of red. The woman stands in a crowd of pedestrians at the intersection of State and Randolph. She is waiting for the light to change.

Maxzyne darts through the crowd. She tugs at the stranger's grimy, red cape from behind.

"Hey, lady! Hey! I need to know her name! What's her name?" Maxzyne shouts above the roar of taxi horns.

The woman doesn't answer.

"You call her something, don't you?"

The woman still does not look at Maxzyne. She pulls her battered suitcase closer to the curb as the pedestrian light flashes white to cross. The crowd moves forward.

"Well, I'm calling her Polly. You know, like polychromatic," Maxzyne continues. "I learned in art class; it means 'lots of colors.' Like the rainbow, or, uh, a kaleidoscope!" She holds out the painting, waiting for the woman to say something.

Finally, the strange woman turns. She touches one of Maxzyne's shiny barrettes. Her brown eyes crinkle around the edges as she gives a half-smile before stepping off the curb.

"Okay, well . . . thank you!" Maxzyne calls after her.

"MAXZYNE!" Mother's shout is clearly angry.

Maxzyne turns to look. Mother stands several yards away, her sunglasses pushed high on her forehead. Her dark eyes blaze. There isn't much time. Maxzyne fumbles with her small canvas bag, fingers searching for the zipper. "Hey, I have to go," she calls to the homeless woman. "But wait—here." Unzipping her purse, she pulls out several dollars. "For the painting—okay?" Suddenly, a city crossing guard blows his whistle, making Maxzyne jump. The green bills flutter to the sidewalk. They land near the woman's scuffed black boots.

"You see that light? It means MOVE, folks!" Blowing his whistle again, the guard waves his arms impatiently.

Maxzyne hops backward on the curb. She carefully rolls up the dog picture until it fits neatly in her hand. Beside her, the woman stoops to pick up the bills, crumpling them into her coat pocket. Seconds before the light changes, the stranger crosses the street. She does not look back once.

"Okay!—so thanks!" Maxzyne calls. "I'll take good care of her—Polly, I mean!" She clutches the painting to her chest. She dashes down the sidewalk toward her mother, whose lips are pressed tight. There are two frown lines between her carefully plucked eyebrows. Maxzyne knows what those lines and the arch of those eyebrows mean.

"Don't even think of doing that again, young lady! Did I just see you give her money?" Mother yanks her owl sunglasses back down over her angry eyes.

Maxzyne hangs her head. Barely nodding, she zips her purse.

"Could there be a more trying child than you! Don't encourage these people, Maxzyne! Besides, you were saving your allowance for a new outfit for your Modern Heroine doll."

"But, Mother! She gave me a picture of the dog! I'm calling her 'Polly' for all the colors she—"

"And I'm calling your father if you ever pull another stunt like that!" She shakes her cell phone under Maxzyne's nose. "You can forget about swimming when we get home, too."

"No way! You said I could break in my new swimsuit. You promised!"

"That was before you decided to run with the homeless," Mother snaps. Under her sunglasses, she pinches the bridge of her nose. She frowns.

"But it's not fair!" Maxzyne protests. "You said—"

"And I said actions have consequences! No, don't argue with me." She rubs her temple again, wincing. "Not now. You've given me a headache."

"I never get to do *anything* fun," Maxzyne grumbles to herself.

Her mother arches an eyebrow over the rim of her sunglasses. Then she thrusts a bag into Maxzyne's hands. "Here. Make yourself useful and show some respect. That's quite enough out of you today," she warns. "We're going straight home, and no more shenanigans. Got that?"

Maxzyne nods. Her bottom lip covers the top one. That's a trick she uses to keep from saying anything more. No sense in making more trouble when she's already *in* trouble. And she knows she's in trouble when Mother starts talking about respect. Grown-ups! What about respect for ten-year-olds? Just because she has her head in the clouds most of the time doesn't mean she shouldn't have some independence. Instead, they're holding her back when she could be growing up!

Silently, they walk the one block home. Under the EL station, they wait for the light to change. Mother looks nervously at the pigeons in the iron rafters. She is afraid of bird droppings. Maxzyne watches two pigeons peck at a pretzel lying in the gutter. She imagines them arguing with each other.

"I saw it first!" the gray bird complains. He hops closer to the pretzel.

"No way! It's mine!" The smaller, brownish-winged pigeon ducks his head. He swoops in for a crumb. The two face each other, flapping and squabbling. Finally the gray bird flies off.

At least you're free to fly wherever you want, she thinks crossly.

A cheery burst of music distracts her from the pigeons. On the far corner, a scruffy old man wearing battered shoes without socks plays an accordion. He is hoping for tips. Maxzyne thinks she must be the only person in the world who can hear him play. Nobody else even looks in his direction. She rocks back and forth on the edge of the curb, daydreaming again. "Maybe he's sending me a secret message. It's in a musical language nobody else understands! What if he's telling the future, or asking for help, or—I know! He's giving me the secret coordinates for the Millennium Park money egg!" Thrilled by this idea, Maxzyne gives the musician a bright smile. It earns her a dip of his stocking-capped head and another glare from Mother. She doesn't dare throw a quarter in the battered case lying open on the sidewalk beside his swollen, red ankles. Instead she turns away, and the music grows slower as the light changes.

Crossing Wabash Street, they continue on Randolph. They pass the silver torch sculpture commemorating 9/11. Then they turn onto Garland Court.

On either side of the entrance to the towering, green glass building where Maxzyne lives, freshly planted purple and yellow pansies dance in the chilly breeze beneath the curved awning. The smell of new mulch, thick and woodsy, fills the air. Mother pushes through the revolving door first. She pretends not to notice when Maxzyne sneaks in an extra revolution. Once inside, the noise of the city is left behind. Jeffrey, the afternoon doorkeeper, rises to greet them from behind the lobby desk.

"Hey there, Maxie! You doing something special for spring break?" He flashes his security card across a panel. It magically opens the glass doors leading to the steel bank of elevators.

Maxzyne skips to the desk, swinging her shopping bag. "Hi, Jeffrey. Umm, we're going to Florida, I guess." She shrugs, fiddling with her purse strap. "Tomorrow."

"You're going to miss that big Easter egg hunt in Millennium Park, aren't you? Heard there'll be $500.00 in one of them eggs, you know. Mayor hid it himself. I just read it in the *Tribune*."

He suddenly notices Mother, waiting at the door. "Oh, hey, need help with those bags, Mrs. Merriweather?"

"No thank you, Jeffrey. And those Easter eggs will be frozen if the weather's anything like today. So we're heading south, where it's warm. Aren't we, Maxzyne?"

"Yeah . . . I guess. Hey, Jeffrey—see what I got?"

"Language, Maxzyne! See what I have," Mother corrects her.

Whatever, Maxzyne thinks, holding up the poodle painting. She is *definitely* not allowed to answer back "whatever" *ever*. That is considered very rude. But sometimes she thinks it. She can't help it. She looks up at Jeffrey. "It's that cool dog in the window at Crowne's. Have you seen it? The one with polka dots?"

"Hey, that's real nice." He nods approvingly. "Did you paint that?"

"No, this lady, she just—"

"Maxzyne Merriweather! What did I tell about needing to get ready for our trip?" Mother sails through the glass doors and into the receiving room to get their mail.

Maxzyne jogs after her. The blue high-tops squeak on polished marble as she waves goodbye to the friendly doorkeeper. "Hope you find the money-egg, Jeffrey! Guess I'll find some sea shells or something at the beach."

"Okay. Bring me back one of them sand dollars. You find one," he calls out, waving back.

The glass door glides shut. Mother holds the elevator door open as the insistent buzzer warns its closing alarm. Clutching the painting, Maxzyne rushes past her. With a grin, she jams her finger on the button for the twenty-first floor.

2

"I Can"

"OKAY. I WANT THAT SUITCASE packed before dinner." Mother hangs up their coats. "Did you hear me?" Maxzyne nods absently. She watches Mother search through the shopping bags. "And don't forget to pack this." Mother hands her the navy swimsuit just purchased from Crowne's Emporium.

Beaming, Maxzyne grabs the new suit. She holds it up, admiring the shining silver anchor on the front. "If I finish packing fast, can I go to the pool? Please? I'll even set the table for dinner first. Can I? Huh?"

"What did I tell you earlier? You lost your chance when you chased after that homeless woman on the street, young lady. And giving her money! What were you thinking? Don't answer that! It's just another example of that imagination of yours causing trouble. With a capital 'T.'" And you know what pressure does to me! This headache means business and so do I. No swimming. I need a nap."

"But I never get to do anything fun!" Maxzyne protests. She flings the swimsuit on the shiny countertop. It slides over the edge and falls to the hardwood floor. "I'm always stuck here! Erika and Gayle are having pizza and popcorn at their sleepover tonight! So how come I'm not old enough?"

Mother points a warning finger. "If you think you're old enough to argue with me, you're growing up too fast already!" She turns away and stalks off to the back bedroom. She groans as she rubs her temples. "Get packed," she orders. "And don't let me hear another peep out of you."

Maxzyne picks up her bathing suit from the floor. "But if I went to the pool I could—"

"What did I just say? You know the condo pool rules—no kids alone under sixteen! What did I say about consequences?" Maxzyne knows better than to argue. She watches the bedroom door close.

With a sigh, Maxzyne swings the suit by its silver straps. Looking at the metallic silver anchor, she rises on her toes, humming softly. "I'm Popeye the sailor man, Popeye the sailor man." *Well, if I was, I'd sail out of here just like those boats racing on the lake every summer,* she thinks crossly. "Ahoy, mate! Anchors away!"

She lays the swimsuit on the countertop. Tracing

a finger around the silver anchor, she thinks out loud. "No way. I'd rather be a mermaid."

Stepping back, she mimes a graceful breaststroke through the air. She circles the kitchen before knocking over a set of stainless steel salt and pepper shakers. Oops. She quickly rights them on the counter, peering down the hall. Luckily, Mother's door is still shut. She grabs the swimsuit. Then she heads down the polished wood hallway, her shoulders slumped. "Better go pack my fins and stuff for Florida."

Inside her bedroom, she throws her swimsuit on the white, four-poster bed and kicks off her sneakers. She glances around the pretty pink and green room. Then she remembers the homeless woman in her ragged red cape. "Even if people are always telling me what to do, I guess it would be pretty scary to be homeless," she mumbles. "And where would you sleep? Or go to the bathroom?" She chews her lip. "That's really scary." She is solemn for a minute. She opens the bedroom closet, takes out her red carry-on suitcase, and unzips it. Better try harder to do what Mother says from now on. She tosses in a pair of flip-flops and returns to the closet. Seconds later, a tennis racket and a bike helmet fly through the air. They each land on the moss-colored carpet.

"So where are my fins?" Frowning, she drops to her knees. She peers under the ruffled bed skirt. Seconds later, she rises, waving a blue swim fin in each hand.

"Score!" she exclaims, sitting on the edge of the bed to strap them on. Straightening her legs, she admires her finned feet.

"Ready for action!" She thinks for a long minute. She turns the fins toward each other. Then she pretends they can talk.

"Can I go to the sleepover?"

"Can't!" the right one answers.

"Can I go to the Easter Egg Hunt?"

"Can't!"

"Can I get my own cell phone?"

"Can't"

"Can I go swim in the pool?"

"Can't!" Maxzyne kicks and flops backwards on the bed.

"Ten years old and all I can do is CAN'T!" she groans.

She raises her legs, doing a lazy frog kick in the air. "Dad says when you've got a problem, break it down. That way, if you think about each part very carefully, you can figure out what to do." She brings the fins together, arching them in graceful sweeps above her head.

"ONE: the indoor pool's just twelve floors down, and I can get there on the elevator. TWO: it's not like I could drown. It's only four feet deep." She crosses and uncrosses her legs in the air. Then she reaches up, trying to touch the fin tips. "THREE: I took swimming lessons last summer. Yes!" She punches the air with her fist. "Give me a break. I can do it!" She waves her finned feet back and forth. Then she flops her legs down on the bed again with a satisfied smile. "Problem solved!"

Rising, she waddles to the window. She leans her forehead against the cold glass. From high above, Millennium Park looks nearly deserted in the late afternoon drizzle below. There is the usual bunch of tourists caught without umbrellas. They crowd together under the stainless steel bean sculpture. She looks out over the horizon. The rippling waves of Lake Michigan call to her. Holding her ear against the glass, she listens, eyes opening wide. "From some distant shore, the mermaid queen hears a call of distress. Help! Help! She must return to her native sea to—to save her best friend from—from . . . I know! Pirates! They're holding her friend prisoner. Don't they know mermaids die if they're out of water?" Maxzyne shakes her head. "Nope. Pirates just want to put her on display and charge people to see the world's first mermaid!"

She backs away from the window. She suddenly kicks off the fins, peels off her clothes and puts on her new swimsuit. She pulls on a lavender robe with oversized, pink buttons that is hanging nearby. Then she throws fins, a beach towel, and swim goggles into a clear, plastic tote bag decorated with neon starfish. She finds her flip-flops in the suitcase and slides into them, wiggling her toes. A pair of sparkly sunglasses completes her aqua costume. Pausing in front of the dresser mirror, she throws her shoulders back. "I'll be a hero and a model!" she decides, pulling the robe sash tight. Arms on hips, she does a runway turn. "And here's Maxzyne, showing our FABULOUS new spring look . . . sporty, yet so, so elegant!" Suddenly, she drops to her knees, peering once more beneath the bed. With a grunt, she squeezes under it. She finally locates her swim cap in the dark.

"Ah-CHOO!" Sniffling and wrinkling her nose, she crawls out, clutching the swim cap. She stuffs it into her tote bag.

"That's everything," she declares. She steps guiltily over the unpacked suitcase. "Oh, wait! No, it isn't!" She dashes back to the foot of the bed, where her beloved Modern Heroine doll sits on a heart-shaped, pink, satin pillow. "C'mon, Faith. Time for adventure. And yes, you can bring a few things." She grabs several small items from the dresser top. "I'll bring your easel, too. You can paint mermaids while I swim, okay?"

Maxzyne tucks the doll, tiny easel, painting board, and paintbrush in her tote bag. Then she makes a final sweep of the room. She scoops a delicate necklace from the dresser, dropping it into a pocket inside the bag. At the last minute, she adds the homeless woman's painting. She carefully rolls and tucks it into the bag next to her doll.

"Don't want to leave Polly behind. She'll keep you company," she reassures the doll. "Hmmm . . . do mermaids have dolls, Faith? She frowns, thinking hard, before shaking her head. "Nah. Just seahorses."

Leaving the bedroom, she steps carefully. However, her flip-flops squeak on the hardwood floor. Mindful of Mother sleeping, she kicks them off and carries them instead. She tiptoes down the long hallway, past the dining room and kitchen, and reaches the condo door. Silence.

"I can!" she whispers, delighted. She grins at her reflection in the huge mirror hanging under the black-shaded chandelier. Then she slides her feet back into the flip-flops and turns the door handle.

3

Elise

HEART THUDDING FURIOUSLY, she opens the door, peering left and right down the hallway. The coast is clear. She steps forward, gently closing the door. Freedom! Marching toward the elevator, she suddenly changes her mind. What if an adult sees her wearing this robe and carrying swim gear? They'll know she's going to the pool alone, and anyone can see she's only ten years old. "Better take the *freight* elevator—almost nobody uses it, except maintenance. That way, nobody can say, 'can't,' right?" She snaps her fingers, pleased to have solved a possible problem.

Quickly backtracking down the hall, she opens the door to another room. Right next to the recycling bin and trash chute is the freight elevator door. Cardboard boxes, neatly stacked beside the blue plastic recycling bins, catch her eye. She presses the down button.

While she waits, she reads box labels.

"A blender—mmmmmm—smoothies . . . books— that reminds me. Better pack that book report I started. It's due when we get back from vacation. What else? A humidifier—boring!" Humming nervously, she swings her bag, willing the elevator to arrive. It would be just her luck to be caught by someone dumping kitty litter or empty boxes. At last, with a whirring noise and gust of warm air, the elevator arrives. The great doors slide open, showing the cold and functional inner space. Although Maxzyne is glad to find it empty, she shivers. She carefully steps in and presses the button for the ninth floor. The doors close and the creaky, metal cage moves downward with increasing speed. She's been on this particular elevator only a few times, helping her mother get holiday ornaments and the artificial tree from their storage space on the eighth floor. "It's sure big in here when you're by yourself," she says. She is shocked when her voice echoes. "Say what?" she asks, shaking. She moves to stand in the center of the car.

"Enough room for warrior pose!" With a quick hop, she quickly gets into the yoga strength position. Closing her eyes, she breathes in, standing calm and balanced. Suddenly, the steel cage lurches, throwing her forward. "Yikes!" she shrieks, grabbing the wall.

"Huh? What's up? Why'd we stop?" She looks at the metal grid overhead and hears hissing coming from somewhere. "Hello? Somebody?"

The hissing noise turns into squeaks and cranking noises. What is it? The elevator car jumps again, shuddering. Worse, the lights buzz and then fizzle out. Her eyes try to adjust to the dark.

"Okay, okay! I don't need to be a mermaid today. No problem—just get me back to twenty-one, please? I'll never leave the condo by myself again." Her whispered promise becomes a wail. "C'mon! Somebody? Help!"

Desperate, she punches buttons, her breath catching in her throat as her stomach churns. Trapped! Where is a grown-up when you need one? In the dark, she searches for a crack in the door, but the elevator lurches again, throwing her off balance. "Mother's going to kill me," she whispers, hanging on to the wall. "And even if she doesn't, I'm grounded for life after this." Sniffling, she swallows hard, trying not to cry.

Without warning, the steel doors grind open, showing a dim, deserted hallway. Bare bulbs in wire cages cast grainy pools of light on the gray floor.

Where am I? she wonders, but the elevator buttons are dark. "No way it's the ninth floor," she declares, punching the buttons again. Nothing. "Okay, I get it! Don't have to tell me twice. I'll take the stairs—just get me out of here!"

Raising the tote bag to her shoulder, she steps out. Nothing looks familiar.

"So where's the exit sign? There have to be stairs,

in case of fire, right?" Hesitating, she looks back at the dreaded elevator. Already, the doors have closed. Biting her lower lip, she winces, feeling a sore spot. Now what to do? "So I'll find the stairs—didn't want to be trapped in the dark again, anyway!" Puzzled, she looks left and right. "Okay, which way?"

"Great," she complains, hitching up her bag and heading left. "Adventure? Looks like I get my wish!" Despite the gloom, she brings her sunglasses down over her eyes just the way Mother does. Striding forward, she doesn't notice when a hidden door silently swings open behind her.

"Over here!" a voice calls out. Turning around, Maxzyne squints in the direction of the voice.

"Hello! This way, please!"

"Who—who's there?" She raises the sunglasses from her eyes. "Hey! Are those the stairs?"

Thrilled, she runs toward a girl her age. Why does she look so familiar? Something about the blonde ponytail, Maxzyne decides. However, she can't quite place her.

"Hurry, I can't

hold him much longer! He's going to get away from me!" the girl pleads.

Reaching the doorway, Maxzyne is shocked to see the girl holding an excited, white, polka dot poodle! "Polly!" she cries, stooping to pat the robin's-egg-blue fur on the dog's wiggling head. The stranger's arms tighten around the excited poodle's neck, trying to contain him. Maxzyne offers her hand, grinning when the dog jumps to lick her cheek. She wipes her face with her sleeve and looks at the girl. "Hey, I know you!" she says. "Yeah, I've seen you before!" She points at the girl's daisy dress. "You're the mannequin in the— wait a minute, how did you . . . ?" She stares at the girl struggling to hold back the excited dog. "No way! But I saw you! I know I did—in the window, today. You were at Crowne's, hiding Easter eggs. It was you!"

Suddenly, the poodle escapes, running between Maxzyne's legs and out the door. With a joyful bark, it scampers down the gloomy hallway. The stranger's lips form a perfect "O" of dismay.

"*Viens ici!*" (Come here!) the girl demands, racing after the dog. "*Garçon mèchant! Viens ici!* (Bad boy! Come here!) Seeing her effort is useless, she stops. "He knows only French," she explains, turning back toward Maxzyne.

"He?" Puzzled, Maxzyne pulls the picture from her tote bag. She presents it to the stranger, declaring, "But I thought 'he' was a 'she' and named her Polly!"

Looking at the painting, the girl laughs. "No, Peppin will never come if you call him that! It would insult his courage—like those silly polka dots they put all over him." She turns, calling after the dog again. "Peppin! *Reviens!*" (Come back!) When the dog does not return she frowns and shrugs. "I'm afraid he's gone exploring for awhile. He never gets out, you know." She quickly taps her daisy headband. "What am I saying? *We* never get out!" Leaning back against the door, the stranger folds her arms across her chest. "At least, not 'til now . . . "

"Well, what happened? Where are we? I was trying to get to the pool and then the elevator went crazy and—"

"—I'm sorry, if we scared you," the girl interrupts. "It was the only way." She looks at the painting in Maxzyne's hand again and points to the smudged initial "E" in the bottom right corner. "Esmeralda gave this to you, but she didn't explain, did she?"

"Who's Esmeralda? And who're you?" Maxzyne demands, her voice rising with each question.

"Esmeralda is the lady who painted Peppin. I saw her give that to you on the sidewalk today." The girl pauses. "And I'm Elise." She offers her hand and is confused when Maxzyne doesn't take it. "A handshake is proper when meeting someone, right? Or if you'd rather this?" Elise leans close, barely touching her lips to Maxzyne's left cheek, then her right, before settling back on her shiny, white Mary Jane heels.

She smiles at Maxzyne's surprised look. "That's the French way! So what's your name?" She watches Maxzyne carefully return the painting to her tote bag.

"Uh—Maxzyne. Maxzyne Merriweather."

"I like that name," Elise tells her. "It sounds strong. And maybe even a little French."

"For sure, not too many girls have an x, y, *and* z in their names! Maxzyne means 'the greatest.' My dad's name is Max, so mine's the girl version—Maxzyne." She lifts her chin, slowly extending her hand. "It even sounds famous, doesn't it?" With a firm squeeze, she shakes Elise's pale hand. "Anyway, Dad says I'm his greatest. Oh, and this is Faith," she adds, pulling the doll from her bag. "Faith Livingston. She's a famous African-American artist—see?" Searching inside the tote bag, she finds the doll's paint set.

"She's beautiful! And she even looks like you!" Elise exclaims.

"Sort of." Under Elise's curious stare, Maxzyne suddenly feels a tiny bit self-conscious.

"All real girls have dolls, don't they?" Elise asks, touching Faith's delicate braids.

"Pretty much. Last summer my aunts took Faith and me to the Modern Heroine store. We watched a video about the real Faith Livingston. She talked about how even when she was a girl my age, she knew she'd be an artist someday. Then we all did a multi-media project together with magazine clippings, fabric, and paint. It was so cool! Wasn't it, Faith?" She looks at her doll, smiling. "Anyway, I picked out a canvas and paints for her, and then we all went to the juice bar for smoothies," Maxzyne finishes.

"You mean there's a place where dolls get to do things as if they were . . . real?" Elise asks in hushed wonder. "Imagine that!" Elise watches Maxzyne secure the doll within her tote bag. Her blue eyes widen when she hears a sudden tinkling sound.

"What's that? Do you hear it? Like a bell ringing?"

"Oh, you mean this?" Maxzyne digs into the pocket of the bag and pulls out a gold chain with a tiny bell. She shakes the chain, and the dainty bell rings softly.

Elise reaches for the necklace. "It's so pretty! But why don't you wear it?"

"I didn't want my mother to hear me when I . . . uh . . ." Maxzyne changes course. "Uh . . . it's special. My Dad brought it back from Switzerland. He says in that country, cows wear bells around their necks so they don't get lost. Anyway, he gave it to me 'cause he thought it might help keep me grounded."

Elise looks confused. "Why does he want you in the ground?"

"Not *in* the ground, silly. Feet on the ground." Maxzyne rises on her tiptoes. "He says I always have my head in the clouds, so this brings me back to earth. Know what I mean?" She lowers her heels back to the floor.

Elise nods uncertainly.

"Adults say I have an overactive imagination." Maxzyne twirls one of her braids, with a wry grin. "I get in trouble at school 'cause I forget to pay attention." She sighs, flipping the braid away from her face. "It's true; I'm always lost in a daydream. Dad says I get sidetracked by the details, stuff nobody else even notices." Maxzyne shrugs. "Guess I'd just rather be on an adventure in my head, instead of where I'm supposed to be." She looks around. "Like right now."

Elise hands the necklace back and watches Maxzyne secure the clasp around her smooth, brown neck. "It's very special. Your father must love you very much." She smiles and then looks down the tunnel in the direction of Peppin's disappearance. Worry flashes across her face. "We better hurry, Maxzyne! I just hope Peppin doesn't get caught sniffing out scraps from Crowne Court garbage cans on the seventh floor."

"Crowne Court? You mean at the café?"

"Yes, of course. The Emporium."

"So where exactly are we, anyway?" Maxzyne's voice drops and starts sounding suspicious. "And why are we in a hurry?"

"We have to find Gigi before it's too late! We haven't got much time, I'm afraid. But first, I'll take you to meet my parents. Maman will want to make certain you can help us." Maxzyne is puzzled. "Help us change Gigi's mind," Elise explains. Suddenly impatient, she takes Maxzyne's arm.

"Wait a minute! Whoa. Like my dad always says, "Let's get all the facts first." Maxzyne pulls her arm back. "Starting with who is Gigi? And who says I want to change her mind? And even if I do, why do you need my help to change it?" she demands. "And you still haven't told me where we are, Elise!" She stomps impatiently on the dusty floor. "I'm not moving 'til I know what's up!"

"Oh! Sorry. I suppose it does sound crazy. Let me explain." Elise squares her shoulders and takes a deep breath. "Okay. First of all, where we are now was once part of a sewing machine factory a long time ago. Lots of old Chicago buildings have tunnels underneath, you see."

"Wow! We're in a secret tunnel?"

"Well, it wasn't always secret! It was used to bring coal and other supplies from the boats on the river and lake. All sorts of things were brought through tunnels like this, making their way into buildings around the city."

"So how'd you find it?"

"Well, as I was trying to explain . . ."

Maxzyne makes a quick "zip" motion across her lips.

Acknowledging the gesture with a nod, Elise

continues. "Years ago, after the factory caught fire and burned down, the property was sold. Crowne's Emporium was built in its place. And sometime after that, we—Maman, Papa, Peppin and I—were purchased from the Parisian Charm Mannequin Company to be their store mannequins." Elise looks proud and then sad. "It was all so wonderful and exciting at first. We were always on display in beautifully decorated windows, always in the latest fashions. People used to make special trips just to see us. Then one year, for some reason, we were put away. They put us in an old storeroom down here, where we seemed to be forgotten." She shudders. "Thank goodness, not long ago, some workers were cleaning up after a flood in the tunnels and found us! Even better, they didn't throw us out! Instead they called the manager of Crowne's, and we were rescued. Everyone had forgotten we existed."

Elise turns, pointing in the opposite direction of Peppin's escape. "And even though I've never been outside, I've learned lots of things after so many years in the store and in the windows. Down that way is the river." She points overhead. "We're under Wabash Street right now."

"Wabash! That's the street at the back of the building where I live!" Maxzyne exclaims. "By the EL station, right?"

Elise nods. "I am sure that is right. I can hear trains

from the window."

"This is so awesome. I live right next door and never knew there was a secret passageway." Thinking hard, Maxzyne frowns. "But this is crazy! You say you've learned things. That you hear things! See things! And, most of all, you're talking to me right now! And you're—well, you're a dummy!"

"Oh, Maxzyne! Never, ever a dummy!" Elise draws herself up. "Please! I am a mannequin. And if you will just be patient, I can explain. Please?" Maxzyne nods, waiting for her to continue. "As I was saying, the tunnel was not secret in the old days. I remember, when we first arrived, they brought us from the boat on the river, here through the tunnel, to the store. Everyone made such a fuss over us! That is, until we got locked away in the dark." She shudders. "Maman says if we hadn't been found soon, the mold could have stained us forever!"

Maxzyne gives a low whistle. "Wow. How lucky that you were discovered! Like finding buried treasure!"

"Buried mannequins, you mean." Elise frowns, smoothing her ponytail. "Anyway, the store manager, Mr. Tracy, says we're just perfect for an old-fashioned trip down memory lane. But our Easter display, the one you saw in the State Street window, is there only until tonight. Because that's when he's—he's . . ."

"Go on. He's what?"

Looking scared, Elise looks at the floor. "He's letting Gigi cut our heads off f-f-for some art exhibit!" Her voice shaking, she touches her neck. Having reassured herself that her head is still attached, she takes a deep breath, her voice cracking. "Now, will you help us?"

"Say what? That's nuts!" Maxzyne is horrified. She tugs on the fine gold chain hanging around her own neck. "He's really going to let this Gigi cut your heads off? I mean, Mother doesn't even let me watch stuff like that on TV! You're making it up, right?"

Shaking her head, Elise fumbles in the pocket of her daisy dress and takes out a printed announcement. "Here. If you don't believe me, read this."

Maxzyne reads out loud.

"*Chicago Art & Design announces HEAD CASE, a contest that will exhibit work based on the representation of the human head in its many forms. Artists working in all media are invited to enter the contest. Finalists will be judged on Saturday, May 19, from 5:00 to 8:00 p.m. Cash awards for the top three artists.*"

Elise slashes a finger across her throat. "Gigi's art needs *our* heads!"

Maxzyne says, "I guess . . . I guess I don't know what to say."

"Say you'll help!" Elise pleads.

"Me! What can I do?"

"You're real. Only a real person can save us from that—that . . ." Unable to speak, she points to the notice in Maxzyne's hand.

"I never saved anyone for real, though." Maxzyne chews her lower lip, thinking. "I want to, but this sounds serious. I mean, I'm only ten."

"Me, too." Elise nods her head, brightening. "I mean, in mannequin years. I'm always ten."

Maxzyne gives a sudden snort of impatience. "Well, this whole thing is just crazy—weird! I'm dreaming, right?"

"What do you mean?"

"Well, how do mannequins walk, talk—in two languages!—but still need me to save them from becoming part of some art exhibit? I'm the 'head case' here!" She waves the art exhibit announcement. "I mean, come on. Everybody knows there's no such thing as, as *real* mannequins!"

"Well, you're talking to me, aren't you?" Hands on hips, Elise glares at Maxzyne.

"Okay, but it's pretty strange, don't you think? Just a little cuckoo?"

"What's more cuckoo than getting your head chopped off?" Elise shoots back.

"Well, I've got to know why you picked me. I really don't get it."

The two girls stand very still, looking at one another. As she thinks over Elise's request, Maxzyne begins folding the dreadful announcement into an origami bird.

"We didn't—Esmeralda did," Elise answers, while watching Maxzyne's quick fingers shape the paper sculpture.

"Huh? That homeless lady?" Maxzyne is doubtful. "She didn't say anything to me. She just ran away."

"Of course. She only talks to us."

"I tried talking to her when she gave me the painting," Maxzyne reminds her.

"She can't talk to real people. She's got something the matter with her—well, I don't remember the word for it. I think I heard Gigi call her 'schizo-something.' When she was decorating our window, her boss, Ray, tried to shoo her away, saying she'd scare off the customers."

"She was a little strange. Definitely scared off my mother!"

"Anyway, when Esmeralda saw you talking to Peppin, I suppose she thought you could help. And then when you ran back and gave her the money, that's when the magic happened! Because ever since that moment, we've been real!" Elise does a little ballet step, her white Mary Janes squeaking on the drab floor.

Maxzyne gives a low whistle. "No way! Magic? Pinch me, I'm daydreaming again, right?" she asks. Then she answers her own question. "Well, except I am talking to you."

"And I'm talking to you. So you'll help us?"

Maxzyne considers. "Well, wait a minute. If you really are real, which you seem to be—why don't you just go tell this Gigi yourself? I mean, seeing is believing, right? She'll see she can't just cut the heads off mannequins who are real."

"But we've never been on our own in the real world. Not like you. Besides, we don't even know how long being real will last. It's never happened before! We only know things from watching and listening and, of course, we can understand each other. But 'til now, we couldn't move, or talk to real people. And we couldn't feel things, like being cold or sleepy. Now everything's different because of the magic! It's like we're free. We can do things. But what if something happens? We could freeze up again, any minute. The magic might wear off, then what?" The mannequin girl shivers.

"It's okay, Elise. I see what you mean." Maxzyne touches Elise's arm gently.

Elise nods, nervously pulling her ponytail. "Anyway, Gigi might not believe me even if I did tell her. Who knows what she'll do? Wait 'til you see her. She's scary—pointy boots, pale white skin and long, straight black hair with red tips. It looks like it's dipped in blood! No wonder she can't wait to cut our heads off." Elise's eyes widen. Grabbing Maxzyne's hand, she pleads, "But she'll believe you, because you're a real girl. And you gave the money to Esmeralda that made the magic. Won't you help us?"

"Of course—I mean, I want to, I'm just not sure if—" Maxzyne looks uncomfortable. Silently, she hands Elise the origami bird.

"It's wonderful! See? You even make things. That means you can make things happen, Maxzyne." Elise slides the folded bird into her daisy pocket.

Maxzyne finally shrugs, nodding. "Whatever happens, it's more fun than waiting for Mother to . . ." Tossing her braids, she quickly changes the subject. "Well, if you can imagine it, you can do it, right?" She swings her tote bag.

"Yes!" Taking Maxzyne's hand, Elise pulls her down the hallway. "And I imagine we better find Maman and Papa right now! Come on, this way!"

Maxzyne pulls the tote bag higher on her shoulder. Maybe she shouldn't have brought all this stuff.

Seconds later, Maxzyne tugs Elise's arm. "Uh, Elise?"

"Yes, Maxzyne?"

"You don't think Gigi would cut the head off a real girl, do you . . .?"

4

Glam Divas

"SO WHERE EXACTLY are we headed?" Maxzyne asks. She struggles to keep up with Elise. Without breaking stride, the other girl races through the gloomy tunnel between the historic department store and Maxzyne's condo building deep underground.

"Trust me," Elise answers. "You'll see."

Maxzyne starts hopping on one foot. She nearly trips. "Owwww!" she screeches, slowing to a stop. "Hold it. My flip-flop broke." Wincing, she rubs her big toe.

Elise picks up the torn sandal. "Here, Maxzyne. Maybe you should just go barefoot. You're wearing a bathrobe anyway."

"It's not a bathrobe! It's a terry-cloth sport robe. I'm wearing it over the latest in swimwear. Check it out!" Maxzyne unties her purple sash and unbuttons the robe, showing her new navy swimsuit underneath. "See? I was on my way to swim!"

"You can swim?" Elise looks at her in wonder.

Maxzyne nods proudly.

"I once saw a florist fall into the fountain while putting up a Christmas display," Elise recalls. "But it didn't look very enjoyable. I don't think she liked getting wet."

"Not unless you're wearing a swimsuit." Maxzyne stuffs her flip-flops into her tote bag. "But you're right. Might as well go barefoot."

"You'll dirty your feet, but I think Maman will insist you find something more practical to wear before meeting Gigi."

Glancing at the concrete floor, Elise quickly strides ahead. Maxzyne follows close behind. A minute later, Elise stops. Her fingers search for something in the gray wall.

"Here it is," she announces, sounding pleased. Leaning against the rough surface, she pushes hard with her shoulder. Much to Maxzyne's surprise, a high, arched doorway appears. It slowly creaks open.

The air greeting them has the stale smell of old, stored things. It reminds Maxzyne of a cluttered antique shop or the attic in her grandmother's house. She sniffs, wrinkling her nose.

Elise shakes the dust from her dress. "Thank goodness! I was afraid it might not let me back in. This way—we're almost there." Elise waves Maxzyne in.

"How'd you find that door, Elise? There's no doorknob or exit sign." This place was definitely creepy and very mysterious. Everything seemed to depend on things that, if not actually magic, seemed pretty magical.

"There is a way to find it—see?" Elise points at the floor. Maxzyne stoops to pick up a small, lace daisy from the dusty concrete. Elise shows her where it was torn from the daisy trim on her dress collar.

"See? I made a little trail to follow. A daisy for every door. So I wouldn't get lost." She pulls the loose threads around the missing trim. "I'm guessing nobody ever sweeps down here. So my daisy might be here forever, unless it floods again."

"What a great idea! Better than Hansel and Gretel, even. And no birds eating crumbs." Maxzyne looks admiringly at Elise. As the hidden door swings back in place behind them, they hear a snuffling, panting noise. It is followed by a high-pitched whine and frantic scratching. Elise rushes to open the door again.

"Peppin! There you are! *Où avez-vous été?* (Where have you been?)"

Peppin bursts through the opening. His brown eyes are wide. He is panting and snuffling. His pink, velvet tongue hangs to one side. His once fluffy fur is now smudged with dirt. His green ribbon dangles loose between his ears.

"Look at you!" Elise scolds. She briskly brushes away the worst of the smudges with her fingers. "Dirt on your polka dots! *Mauvais chien!* (Bad dog!) Better hope Mr. Tracy doesn't see that. Or Maman!"

Peppin wags his tail. He gives two short barks and a high-pitched whine. Alarmed, Elise quickly slams the door closed. "Ugh! Peppin says there are big rats living in the tunnels and they chased him back. We better move fast." Maxzyne's mouth drops open in disbelief.

"Wait! He told you that? He talks?"

"I told you. He speaks French. Why do you look so surprised? You were trying to talk to him earlier today in the window. Weren't you?"

"But that was kind of, well, pretend. You can understand him when he barks, growls, whines, whatever?"

"Of course. We've been together a long time. He was good company all those years we were forgotten in the storeroom."

"Talking dogs, secret doors—awesome! This adventure gets better and better." Elise moves forward. Maxzyne rushes to catch up. "Hey! Think you can teach me a little French sometime, Elise? I mean, I only know some Spanish from school. Please? It would be so cool. And I've never talked to a dog. At least not for real."

Elise walks quickly, searching the floor for her secret trail. "I will. I promise. After you take care of

Gigi for us." She stops suddenly, spotting another daisy marker. She pushes on another door. Peppin rises on his hind legs to help her. "*Merci,* Peppin." Elise smiles, stepping aside. The door swings open, and she lets the dog run ahead. "This is the last one, Maxzyne—we're in the store basement now."

The musty smell of old things is stronger now. Peppin scampers toward a winding, old-fashioned iron staircase. He snuffles furiously. Boxes, hangers, racks of clothes, silk flowers, shoes, and hats are stacked in piles that reach to the ceiling. Frames, posters, baskets, along with shimmering bolts of fabric and ribbon, overflow the shelves. On a nearby metal table, shears and wire cutters rest beside rolls of paper. A faint, waxy smell, like melted candles, is in the air. Maxzyne reaches for a black glue gun. With a fierce look, she points it at Elise.

"Don't move, or I'll shoot!"

Elise freezes. "What . . . ?"

"Kidding!" Grinning, Maxzyne returns the glue gun to its stand on the oversized table. "Geez, you *are* jumpy, aren't you?"

"Huh! Of course I knew it wasn't real." Elise points across the table a little huffily. "Like those birds over there."

Maxzyne steps closer to examine a fancy birdcage. She squints at the dusty pair of stuffed parakeets inside.

"Ahhh-chooooo!" From several yards away, Peppin sneezes. Then he gives a quick bark.

"He says, *'Excusez-moi! Pardon!* (Excuse me! Pardon!)'" Elise translates.

"Hey, that's French I already know," Maxzyne giggles. "Bless you, Peppin!" She follows the dog up the iron steps, taking them two at a time. Halfway up, she sees something out of the corner of her eye and freezes. In the dim light of a single, hanging bulb, she can see something is there! Her skin crawls. What is it? Ducking below the banister, she catches Elise by surprise.

"What is it? Is someone there?"

Nodding silently, Maxzyne rises to peer over the banister. She points to a huge shadow on the far wall. From her point of view, the shadow looks like an army of men standing at attention. But something is weird. The soldier heads are bare, and their stiff bodies have narrow waists and oversized shoulders. Afraid to move, Maxzyne looks at Elise. "What are they?" she whispers.

Elise holds back a giggle. "Those are just Chromatones, Maxzyne. Our replacements—no faces, no hair, and definitely no feelings." She casts a withering glance toward them. "Those things, well, you can call *them* dummies anytime. They're horrible!"

Reassured, Maxzyne rises for a better look. The blank, featureless faces are freaky.

Elise grips the railing, rocking on her heels. "Mr. Tracy says it's the look of the future." She sniffs scornfully. "One step above clothes hangers, don't you think? But they're getting rid of us, because everybody wants something new." She glares at the shadowy army. "Like fake is better."

"Creepy," says Maxzyne. "Wouldn't want to meet them in a dark hallway or—"

From the stairs above, Peppin whines impatiently. "*Tais toi* (Hush), Peppin!" Elise scolds him. "We don't want Mr. Tracy to find us, do we?" Peppin claws the metal step in response. "All right! We're coming." Elise scurries up the stairs.

Maxzyne hurries after Elise. When they reach the top, Peppin sniffs and suddenly sneezes again.

"*Santé!* (Bless you!) It's the main floor, Maxzyne. These stairs lead to the back of the cosmetics department. You know, I think Peppin is allergic to perfume now that he is real. He's always sneezing!"

"Can't blame him. I sneeze, too, when those ladies try to spray that smelly stuff on me or Mother!"

"Oh, but I love being able to smell the French perfumes. And all the fresh spring flowers, too." Elise smiles dreamily.

"Hey, Elise! Earth to Elise!" Maxzyne gives Elise's arm a quick jab as they climb the last three steps. Unnerved by the bright light, they stop for a moment. Overheard, the soaring skylight makes the huge store seem especially enormous and vaguely threatening. Maxzyne suddenly feels overpowered by the energetic hum of business: snippets of conversation, footsteps on marble, rustling of bags, faint music, and even horns blaring outside in traffic. It's like a foreign world without Mother. Luckily, Elise is used to it. "Where to?" Maxzyne asks.

Crouching low, Elise peers through the iron rails of the old-fashioned staircase. "Well, so far I don't see Mr. Tracy anywhere."

"Good. We better look normal now, in case someone notices us," Maxzyne whispers. She pulls the fluffy towel from her tote bag and wipes the fine, gray dust from her hands. Offering the towel to Elise, she points at the girl's pale cheek.

"You've got a dirt smudge. Right there." Elise grabs the towel. She rubs hard, making her cheek turn bright pink. "Okay, okay. You got it already," Maxzyne assures her.

"Can you carry Peppin in that bag?" Elise rolls up the towel. "I'm afraid he'll give us away. They don't allow real dogs in the store. Unless you need their help, of course."

"He's kind of big. But if you carry Faith, he might fit." Maxzyne hands over her Modern Heroine doll, partially wrapping her in the towel. Looking very serious, Elise holds Faith tight, fearful of dropping her.

"No, not like that! She's no baby doll; she's a

famous artist! Like me, someday." Maxzyne shifts the doll to a standing position in the crook of Elise's right arm. "There. Now she can see stuff. An artist needs to look around, you know."

"You're nice to think of your doll that way, Maxzyne."

"What way?" Maxzyne is confused.

"Well . . . like she's the same as us. Or, er, us since the magic made us real," she corrects herself. She smoothes the doll's shining braids.

Satisfied that Faith is in good hands, Maxzyne kneels and urges Peppin to jump into the tote bag. He sniffs scornfully and backs away.

"Peppin! *Monte!*" (Get in!) Elise orders, pointing. With a low growl, he unwillingly steps into the tote. Once he's secure, Maxzyne puts the handle over her shoulder. She grunts at the extra weight. Elise strokes Peppin's now dusty face. She smiles reassuringly at him between the handles, but he only groans.

"Okay, when we get into the light, just pretend we're store models. You know, showing the latest stuff for spring," Maxzyne suggests. She smoothes her terry robe. "How's my hair?" She fluffs her braids, expert fingers checking barrettes.

Elise nods. She smoothes her own ponytail and pulls the elastic band with its decorative daisy tighter. Suddenly she gasps and punches Maxzyne hard on the arm.

"Oww! What's up? Did someone see us?"

"There's Mr. Tracy over by the fountain, talking with Gigi! Oh, no! I have to get back to the window before they see I'm gone!"

"Wait a minute! Don't panic! My dad's a trader at the Chicago Merc, and he says you can lose your shirt if you panic."

Elise looks confused. "You can?"

"Well, not really. It's just a way of saying if you panic bad things can happen. A figure of speech. You can also say, 'chillax' or 'be cool.'"

"Chill what?"

"Chill-ax! It's like chill plus relax. Get it?"

Elise nods. "Okay, I get it. Don't worry. I'll get better at being real!"

"You're doing great. Now where'd you see him? Which one is Mr. Tracy?"

"He's the one over there. With the mustache." Elise points. "See? And the bow tie. Oh, no! There's Gigi! See the girl with long hair wearing scary high boots? Quick! Follow me." They trot forward. "Okay. Behind here." They duck behind a bronze screen that is fashioned in a grid of climbing vines and acts as a kind of divider.

The two girls peer through a convenient chink in the metal screen at a frowning, red-faced man wearing a pink shirt and purple bow tie. He is standing by a huge floral display. He points angrily at some drooping branches of forsythia where tall, golden stalks have fallen into the blue hyacinths. A tall woman, with straight black hair bleached white at the ends and tipped with blood-red, rearranges the forsythia. The girls watch nervously as the creepy-looking woman turns. Her dark, almond-shaped eyes flash when the store manager points to his watch and the fallen flower stalks, his face growing redder by the second.

Maxzyne is unnerved by the sight of Gigi. She wonders how a ten-year-old could ever convince someone like that of anything. Then her attention is drawn back to the store manager. "Mr. Tracy looks like he has one bad headache," she whispers to Elise. "Geez. If he acts like that all the time, no wonder she wants to cut the heads off stuff."

"From what I hear, he gives everyone who works here headaches. So what do we do now?"

"We have a plan, remember? We're live models. It's show time."

Elise looks sick.

"Hey! They're not going to recognize you. Grown-ups are too . . . well, they never notice the details, and they've got no imagination," Maxzyne reassures her. "So just act like—"

"—a mannequin. I mean a real model," Elise interrupts, swallowing hard. "And—I know. Chillax!"

"You got it!" Maxzyne tucks a flyaway braid behind one ear. "Play it safe, though. Don't go too close to Mr.

Tracy or Gigi. Or any adults! Just in case."

Alarmed at the thought, the girls gravely nod together. Each reaches for the other's hand, takes a deep breath, and squeezes. They step out into the bustling showroom, heads held high.

Elise sneaks a look at the glittering, tiled ceiling dome. She counts the levels of floors soaring above their heads. Then she stops, spellbound. Maxzyne tweaks her ponytail from behind. "Hey!"

"I never realized how beautiful it was in here. Realizing! Do you think that's a part of being real?"

"Realize this, Elise! Focus!" Maxzyne hisses.

Makeup artists buzz around them, holding mirrors, answering questions, and applying brushes and powders to faces old and young, fat and thin, eager and bored. Registers spew out sales slips. Smocked clerks get out mysterious boxes of potions, tubes of creams, lipsticks, and eye shadow from shelves and display cases. The two impostors pass the Glam Diva Maquillage counter. A young woman debating lipstick shades catches sight of them in her mirror. Smiling, she turns around. "Well, don't you look adorable? I didn't know they were using live models in the store, did you?" she asks the heavily made-up sales clerk assisting her. The clerk, wearing a trim, navy smock, with the name "Barbara" in gold script on the pocket, offers up a fresh cotton ball dipped in makeup remover.

"No, I didn't." Barbara glances at the fake models as the customer scrubs various shades of lipstick from where she's tested them on her wrist. "Hmmm . . . I think they could use some color on those cheeks, don't you?" Holding up a gold-handled brush and royal blue compact of rouge, she waves the girls over. "How about some Coral Bisque, young ladies?" Her mascaraed eyelashes flutter as she surveys the two from head to toe. She looks slightly puzzled when she notices Maxzyne's bare feet.

"Yes, please." Maxzyne steps forward. She hopes the woman doesn't ask about her bare feet. Elise joins her at the counter. They raise their faces to the light as Barbara skillfully sweeps the soft brush across their cheekbones.

"Perfect. And maybe some gloss on those rosebud lips, too?" The clerk holds a mirror to Maxzyne's face. *Wow, pretty sophisticated for someone who's not even allowed to go to a sleepover,* she thinks.

Peppin sneezes. Heads turn in surprise.

A young woman points at Maxzyne's bag. "Oh, look! They've got a little dog! Just like the one I saw in the window! How sweet!" she gushes.

"My goodness! Visual advertising is really going over the top for the spring flower show this year, aren't they?" Barbara lets the mirror clatter to the counter. She peers at Peppin's half-hidden face. "Ladies! Yoo-hoo, ladies! Come see the models!" she urges the other clerks. A small crowd gathers as Barbara applies a layer of pale, shimmery gloss to each girl's puckered lips.

"Now do this," she instructs, pressing her own lips together. They do as they are told. "Wow!" Maxzyne looks at Elise. "Flavored lip gloss! How cool is that?"

"Tastes like lemon, doesn't it?"

"Mmmm." They try not to lick their lips.

"It's called 'Citrine Diva,' girls. Should be the hottest gloss in our spring collection, if you want to help promote it. Oh, by the way. What agency did you say you were with?"

Maxzyne pretends not to hear. She bends over the bag where Peppin whines from between the tote's plastic handles. "Shhhhh!" she says. "We'll let you out soon, boy." She reaches for Elise's hand. "Let's get going," she mutters. The girls edge toward the towering flower display in the center of the store.

But the chattering crowd around them cuts off their escape. "Look at these adorable kids!" Smiling, a short woman in a pink smock searches her pocket. "I think I've got some yellow ribbon to match those daisies. Here!" Waving it, she approaches Elise.

"Oh! Marketing genius!" another squeals.

"So creative, using actual children!" A large-breasted woman wearing a tag that reads "Department Manager" nods approvingly. Her black glasses magnify her thick brown eyeliner and huge false lashes.

"Oooh, let me try a little of this on you." A thin woman in black pants and a white T-shirt, with the brand name *Beau Ideal* (Ideal Beauty) in swirling crimson, pushes Elise toward the mirror. Elise timidly gazes at her reflection. Her eyes meet Maxzyne's as the cosmetics clerk shades her pale eyebrows with a small brush.

"You'll love our new hair shimmer product. Amazing stuff. Have a spray," someone else urges. She wildly spritzes their hair with an aerosol can.

Each clerk fights to apply her particular product to the girls' hair and faces. Not even Faith, the doll, is spared. Caught in a cosmetics whirlwind, the girls are helpless to resist until a generous splash of sweet, jasmine perfume offends two sensitive noses.

"Ah-choo!" Maxzyne sneezes loudly. Peppin echoes her, poking his head out from between the tote bag handles. One paw rubs his offended nose. A burst of delighted laughter ripples through the crowd.

"Well, bless you!" proclaims the woman in pink,

bending toward the dog. He squirms as she tries to fasten a plush pink and gold ribbon around his neck. Barbara smoothes his ears with a tiny comb. "We could put some polish on those precious toes, too," she coos, giving him an air kiss.

"That's brilliant! A French manicure for a French poodle!" the pink lady crows. Peppin whimpers. Ducking his head, he burrows deeper into the tote bag.

"I think he's had enough, but thank you, ladies!" says Maxzyne.

"Yes," Elise adds. "Sorry. He's a bit shy."

"We better get back to work." Maxzyne smiles nervously at the crowd, stepping away. She pokes Elise. "Nod and smile," she mutters through clenched teeth.

Elise flashes a smile, stepping backward. Maxzyne shifts the tote bag to her other shoulder, out of range of the pink lady's clutches. The two girls slowly back away from the crowd at the counter.

"Thank you everyone," Elise says, waving. She adds, "But Mr. Tracy expects us mannequins, er, models to move the stock!" She looks at Maxzyne.

"Right! So sorry! Got to get going!"

"Well, come back for a touch-up during your break, girls," calls the Department Manager.

"Yes, do! And if anyone asks, your favorite lip gloss is Citrine Diva," Barbara urges. She hands Maxzyne a small bottle. "Here! Take these samples for your mothers. Are they here today? They must be so, so, so proud of you! And don't forget, my name's Barbara!"

"Okay. Bye, now!" The girls melt into the crowd swirling toward the Grand Hall. Maxzyne hears the fountain gurgling in the center. She forgets Elise for a moment. She glances at the balconies of the other floors stacked overhead and at the escalator marching up toward the soaring glass atrium. Her head spins. The huge space makes her feel small. How can she save anyone? *This adventure is bigger than any I've ever dreamed up at home,* she thinks. Her chest tightens. "Breathe," she whispers.

Elise approaches the fountain. She glances nervously around for Mr. Tracy or Gigi. Around them, people get on and off the escalators, jostling the girls where they stand. People turn to stare.

"Uh oh. Where to now?" Maxzyne whispers to Elise. "We're stopping traffic. We need to get out of here! People are staring at us."

"They're supposed to stare. We're mannequ—I mean models, remember? Just stare back." Elise nudges Maxzyne. "Like this." She flashes a smile, turning gracefully. People stop and start forming a circle around them.

"Got it." Maxzyne raises her chin and imitates Elise. Smiling, she puts the heavy tote bag higher on her shoulder. She ignores Peppin's growls.

"So how do we get from here to your window? Maybe it's just the polka dots, but Peppin's getting heavy already."

"This way." Elise turns left. She weaves through a chattering crowd of ladies waving red-dot sales coupons.

"It's over here. By the State Street entrance at the corner of Randolph, remember? Just follow me."

They stride confidently past the fountain. The fresh smell of chlorinated water mingles with the fragrant hyacinths and lilies. Tourists snap photos of the magnificent arrangement as Elise steps around them. She heads into the costume jewelry department.

Maxzyne is quickly distracted by a white wooden screen overflowing with ivy and pink orchids. Tiny, jeweled hummingbirds hover near the blossoms, cleverly fastened with slender wires. She can't resist touching one. The movement sets off a chain reaction. The fluttering birds positively hum. "Cool! That's so awesome!"

Grinning, she looks over the goods displayed below the graceful trunk of a plum tree in full bloom. Costume jewelry glitters. It is arranged in pink and black boxes shaped like old-fashioned steamer trunks. She sighs, soaking up the magic. Suddenly, her heart thumps as she searches the crowd for a familiar face. Elise! Where is she? Weaving through the crowd, Maxzyne spots her waiting in a far corner. She rushes over, guilt pricking her conscience. "Earth to Maxzyne!" she scolds herself.

Elise stands beside a velvet curtain. "Where were you?" she demands, adjusting her headband. "I was so worried! I thought—"

"Sorry!" Maxzyne gives an apologetic shrug. "My fault. Those hummingbirds were just too cool. Did you see them? And that jewelry!"

Elise gives an impatient snort. She turns to search for an opening in the curtains. "I just hope Maman and Papa are still—Maman?" Pulling aside the fabric, she disappears. In a flash of polka dots, Peppin springs out of Maxzyne's tote bag. He skitters through the curtain with a final wave of his lavender tail.

5

Aloin & Veronique

MAXZYNE HEARS A muffled flurry of French and English from beyond the curtain folds. She suddenly feels shy. Will Elise's parents like her? True, they need her help, but will these mannequin adults take her seriously? Or will they be like most adults, having little patience for a ten-year-old with an active imagination? She curls her dusty toes. Squaring her shoulders, she smoothes her robe, reties the sash neatly around her waist, and straightens her braids. *And don't forget to breathe,* she reminds herself. She takes a deep breath just as Elise calls for her.

"*Entre* (Come in), Maxzyne! They're here."

Heart fluttering, Maxzyne peeks in. Here it is! The store window she was admiring just this afternoon. The adult mannequins are still posed as they were earlier, but Elise kneels on the carpet now. Her back is to the window.

"Did anyone notice I was gone, Papa?"

Maxzyne notices that Faith has been placed on the antique cabinet.

Elise picks up a golden egg from the plush Oriental carpet by the chair.

"No, we were very lucky. Is that not so, Veronique?" With a flick of his head, Elise's father signals her to return to hiding eggs with Peppin in the window. Elise scoots into her proper pose by the chair. She pretends to scold Peppin, but he yawns. Then he sits down with a loud thump.

"I think being a real dog has exhausted him," Elise laughs.

Maxzyne enters. She prefers to remain hidden in a curtain fold. She instantly recognizes the tall lady mannequin with ash-blonde hair swept forward in a graceful wave. This must be Veronique, Elise's "Maman." The elegant woman wears a lilac, silk dress trimmed with pearl buttons. On her narrow feet are stylish, ivory pumps. Maxzyne smiles uneasily, feeling the adults' scrutiny. They look at her from the corners of their eyes, careful to remain in their poses. Worse, she can tell Veronique is noticing her casual robe and bare feet! Veronique's long eyelashes flutter as she glances outside. Realizing the sidewalk in front of their window is momentarily empty, the elegant lady suddenly moves. She sinks gratefully into a Chippendale chair.

"Aloin—I must rest. *Mon Dieu!* (My goodness) It's exhausting to stand in one place so long now that we are made real. Please, *cheri* (dear), take a seat for a moment while no one watches!"

"I am fine, my dear. Not tired at all. And I must welcome our friend." Elise's father turns to nod in Maxzyne's direction.

"*Bonjour, mademoiselle!* (Good day, miss!)" He glances out the window. Then he hurries to where Maxzyne stands by the curtain, reaches for her hand, and kisses it. Just as quickly, he returns to his pose.

Maxzyne quickly recovers from her surprise and pleasure at the hand-kiss. She nearly giggles when a pedestrian pauses to stare. He finally shakes his head in disbelief and moves on.

"You'll get us caught, *mon cher* (my dear)," Veronique scolds, barely moving her lips. "Please, take care!"

"My darling, Veronique! Allow me to finally give you this Easter basket I've been holding forever. The champagne is warm, but the chocolates, I must admit, are divine," he says guiltily. "*Oui,* I did sample one when nobody was looking. Forgive me for not sharing earlier. Now I understand their fascination with food, my dear. It's even better than I imagined!"

"*Merci* (Thank you), *mon cher.*" She glances out the window before popping the chocolate into her mouth. "Oh, it is true! Most delicious!"

Elise interrupts. "Maman, you remember Maxzyne, don't you? She was outside earlier today with Esmeralda."

"*Oui*, of course, I remember," Veronique answers. "I see everything that happens in our window to the world." She quickly turns a critical blue eye on Maxzyne. Then she snaps back to her pose. "But was she not dressed more *approprié* (appropriately) earlier?"

The heat rushes to Maxzyne's face. She wants to shrink deeper into the curtain. Maxzyne curls her dirty toes, chewing the sore spot on the inside of her bottom lip.

"My dear, what is this, this *peignoir* (robe)? Why, it's much too casual to wear in public! And no shoes! How will she ever convince Gigi to spare us, looking so unprepared? *Non*, I think she is too young to help."

Maxzyne's cheeks burn. Adults. She can't get a break. Not even from a mannequin!

Aloin gives Maxzyne a smile. "Don't mind Veronique, child. She is partial to the glory days of fashion, I suppose. With a bit more, how shall I say . . . *savoir faire* (sophistication), my dear?" Smiling wryly, Aloin looks at his wife.

"I am only partial to looking my best, as all French *femmes nobles* (ladies) do!" Veronique's eyes flash.

Chuckling, Aloin lovingly touches her high cheekbone.

"*Ma cherie*, you forget. We are from Milwaukee, Wisconsin." He checks the window. Then he quickly sits down in the remaining chair, sighing with relief.

"*Fabriqué* (Made) by the Parisian Charm Mannequin Company!" his wife pouts. "I am a French mannequin!"

"We are French in name only, remember? Although I'm afraid years of fittings with Babette, the seamstress, certainly made us feel French, *ma cherie*," he concedes. "But even a French poodle, like our very own Peppin, was made in a Wisconsin factory right here in America."

"*Oui*, Aloin. And this dress was made in China," she retorts. "But the label? 'French Fever!' See for yourself!" Veronique takes out the tag from under her sleeve. She holds it for him to read.

He chuckles. Seeing the sidewalk is again empty for the moment, he leans over to squeeze his wife's arm lovingly.

Elise holds back a laugh. She rolls the egg to Peppin, waking him. He sniffs scornfully. He looks longingly instead at the macaroon-filled Easter basket. Veronique notices and pushes it away with a pointy shoe.

"Even the dog has a nose for fine French pastry," she says. Peppin sighs, closing his eyes as she smiles at him. "Peppin, only you and I appreciate all that is fine and French, *non*?"

"Maman, Maxzyne was on her way to swim when I found her," Elise interrupts. "That's why she's dressed this way. It's not her fault."

"*Nager*? (Swim?)" Veronique stares at Maxzyne. "You can swim, child?"

"Of course! I took lessons."

Astonished by this news, Veronique turns to her husband. He shrugs, startling a young couple walking past the window. Maxzyne shrinks deeper into the curtain fold. The mannequins pause. They wait patiently while the spectators argue over whether they saw something move. Still puzzled, the couple finally wanders off.

"You swim in the lake?" Veronique looks doubtful. "*Non*, I do not believe you. It's so *froid*—cold—yet. Wearing this silk frock, I can feel the chill through the glass when the sun hides behind the tall buildings in the afternoon."

"Oh, not in the lake. I only swam in Lake Michigan once with my Dad last summer. I swim in our pool. It's inside our building. On the ninth floor," Maxzyne explains. "I wanted to try out my new swimsuit since we're going to Florida tomorrow. But then Mother wouldn't . . . uh . . ."

She breaks off. But Elise smiles, encouraging her to continue. "Well, anyway, she had a bad headache and I didn't want to wake her. So I took the freight elevator, but it didn't stop at nine, even though I pushed the button. For the pool, I mean. Then the lights went out, and there was this loud crashing noise right before the elevator fell and I was trapped! That is, 'til the door finally opened into the secret tunnel, and I met Elise," she finishes, nearly out of breath.

"See, *cherie* (darling)? This child is quite courageous and independent. Surely she can help us. In or out of water."

"Because she's a real girl. Real girls can do anything, Maman."

"Do you really think so, child?" Veronique looks at Maxzyne. "You can convince Gigi to let us keep our heads?"

Maxzyne nods. She steps out from the curtain fold. "Uh . . . sure. Besides, if she's an artist, like my favorite teacher, Ms. McCarthy, she's cool, right?" Maxzyne grins, forgetting her robe and dusty toes. "Anyway, next to art, my favorite thing's adventure!"

Veronique's eyes narrow. "But this adventure requires a change of clothes, *mademoiselle.* Gigi cannot be convinced if you're wearing sleepwear—*non*—swim clothes, to be sure," she declares.

"We can go upstairs to the girls' department, Maxzyne! You can find something to wear on Level Four," Elise offers. "I'll help you!" Excited, she rolls the golden egg too hard. It spins across the carpet. Aloin quickly stops it with his shiny, leather shoe.

"Not so fast, *ma petite* (my little one)! You are

needed in this window. Have you forgotten? We don't know how long this 'being real' will last. And when it stops," he shakes his head, looking grave, "I need to know you are safe here with us."

"But I've spent my whole life watching everyone else through windows, Papa! Or worse, locked in storage!" Elise cries. "I have to go with her! Please! No one will notice. We'll be just a few minutes. Say I can."

Her outburst wakes Peppin from his nap at Veronique's feet. "No, you stay!" Elise tells him. "*Reste ici!* (Stay here!)" Peppin whimpers, thumping his tail.

"I'll bring Elise right back, Mr. French," Maxzyne promises. "We'll keep pretending to be floor models, so no one will guess what we're up to," she offers. "We got here okay, didn't we?" Elise nods excitedly.

"And once I find something to wear," Maxzyne continues, "I'll find Gigi. I'll just go right up to her and explain why she can't make you part of her—her, uh . . ."

"Head Case exhibit," Aloin offers. Elise cringes. She frowns at her father.

"Don't worry, Mr. F.," Maxzyne reassures him. "I'll bring Elise back here first. I promise." Sounding a bit more confident than she feels, she adds, "Then I'll go find Gigi and convince her by myself."

Aloin looks at his wife. "*Cherie?*"

Veronique's full, ruby lips turn down, but she nods. "*Oui.* I will allow it this time," Aloin agrees. "But you will return quickly, Elise. You will be gone only a few minutes. Understand?" Beaming, Elise nods.

"You must take great care, *mes enfants* (my children)," Veronique warns. She suddenly shivers. "Perhaps you might find a shawl for me? I have such strange bumps from the cold. The chill air makes it difficult to stay still," she complains, rubbing her arms.

"I promise I'll be careful and come right back, Maman," Elise reassures her. "And I'll find a shawl, too."

Maxzyne pulls the heavy, white curtain aside. "Nice meeting you. We fashionistas will be right back."

"Just remember, being real brings opportunity for real trouble, Elise."

Elise rises. She is grateful that a disturbance at the intersection outside has distracted the pedestrians. At that moment, a woman in a threadbare, red cape comes forth from the crowd at the corner. She carries a worn suitcase. She makes a beeline for the window, waving to the mannequin family from the other side of the glass.

"There's Esmeralda!" Elise exclaims, pointing. Peppin rises, barking.

"*Chut!* (Hush!)" the family warns together.

Elise leans on the glass. She strains to hear the homeless woman. "We have to hurry! Esmeralda says she overheard Gigi make a call earlier. It was over by the worker entrance, where people sometimes give her coffee. Gigi asked a friend to bring his truck to pick us up after work tonight." Elise pauses, listening carefully. "Oh, no! Gigi gets our heads, but she's promised the rest of our body parts to, to—to the friend in exchange for his help!"

Veronique's face flushes pink. Then it goes pale. Her eyelashes flutter, and she looks as if she might faint. Alarmed, Aloin squeezes her arm. "All is not yet lost, *cherie*. You must calm yourself. Maxzyne will help us."

Elise turns to Maxzyne, pleading. "You've got to tell Gigi she can't do this! Why it's—it's murder!"

"You're right, Elise. Come on!"

Maxzyne slips through the white curtain. She lets it fall in place behind her. Her stomach churns as she tries to calm her jitters with a few deep breaths. Elise joins her and the girls stand gazing at the enormous store with its polished marble floors, distracted customers, harried clerks, and glittering goods. Maxzyne gives Elise's hand a reassuring squeeze, thinking: *I'm responsible now. I promised to help.* She bites her lip, wincing when she hits the sore spot. *This is more than an adventure. It's a chance to prove I can!* She turns to Elise. "Don't forget. We're store models again. Get your game face on."

"It would be a game if it wasn't so real!" Elise nervously smoothes her blonde ponytail and adjusts the daisy headband. "But I do like being a model much more than being a mannequin. Even more, I love being a real girl. You're so lucky, Maxzyne!"

The girls head back toward the spring display and the Grand Hall escalators. Looking past the fountain, Maxzyne elbows Elise. "Just stay away from cosmetics. Those ladies are crazy!"

6

Gigi

BACK TO BEING PRETEND models, the girls strut across the sales floor. As they head toward the escalators, Maxzyne notices the crowds have dwindled. Luckily, they don't attract as much attention. As they approach the fountain, with its towering floral display in the Grand Hall, Elise gasps.

"What's up?" Maxzyne whispers nervously.

"It's Gigi! And Ray. Right in front of us. See them? Over there on the other side of the fountain." Elise jerks her chin in that direction.

"Quick! Under here. Let's spy on them. That way, if we need to, we can change our plan."

Maxzyne and Elise duck, wriggling behind a flower-covered screen near the fountain. Several feet away, Gigi and Ray wind ribbons around pots of pink orchids.

"You know what?" Gigi asks. "I'm starting to really hate forsythia. They're yellow, they droop. And their stupid pollen gets everywhere. I think the Tracy-monster's evil eye scares them!" She picks up several of the fallen stalks, unaware of the two girls watching her from behind.

"Oh, I know that evil eye! Too well!" Ray answers.

Maxzyne and Elise hold their breath as Ray's shoes pass inches from their hiding place. Peering from the greenery, they watch him lift another orchid in place.

"I'm keeping a lookout," Ray assures her. "We don't need him freaking out again."

"Yeah, well keep a lookout for the guy from payroll! I need my check, so those mannequins Tracy promised me will be mine to slice and dice tonight!"

"Seems a shame, cutting them up like that. I mean, they're a part of history, when you think about it." He wanders further away, calling back. "Should be in a museum or something. Like you, Goth Girl."

"Get with the times, Ray. Display is going high tech. Futuristic. Can't stop progress."

"I'm sorry, kid, but those Chromatones don't really do it for me. Too cold. Unnatural. It's not a look I like."

"Hey, displays will be nothing but holograms soon.

Or video on giant flat screens. Sometimes I wonder if people even notice what we do, us merchandise magicians, working behind the scenes. How much longer can we keep tempting them to buy stuff?" She steps back, shrugging. "Anyway, what do you think? All fixed now?"

Ray's shoes return. "Perfect. You do good work, even if your ice cold heart lets you chop off classic heads!"

Elise gasps. Maxzyne gives her a warning pinch.

"Recycling for art!" Gigi retorts.

"Oh, that's what you're calling it now?"

"Sure. Thanks to you, boss. And all the hours you let me work, so I can buy art supplies, cappuccino, and now those mannequin heads."

"Yup. Still time for you to have a change of heart."

"Speaking of hearts, Ray, yours is a melting marshmallow, just oozing for a girlfriend."

"Huh?"

"You know. It's time you had someone special to hang with. Like maybe Ms. Mitchell from girls' clothing? I've seen you jump chairs to sit by her at meetings."

Maxzyne elbows Elise, grinning. *Bet he's blushing,* she thinks.

Ray gives an embarrassed cough. "Come on, Gigi!"

"I mean it, Ray! Life's short."

"Yeah, well, time's short, too. Let's get the stuff on

my cart over to that window we're redoing since you're claiming those mannequins. Don't want to spend all night here."

"Got it. And, yes, I did notice that you changed the subject, boss."

"I changed the subject because here comes trouble with a capital 'T.' Our boss!"

Alarmed, the girls shrink deeper into the leaves. Elise reaches for Maxzyne's arm and squeezes hard.

"Well, well," says a high, nasal voice. Curious to see the manager from up close, Maxzyne squints through the greenery. "I see you've finally fixed the flowers. I need you both to be more productive. We've got deadlines."

"You've got, it, Mr. Tracy! Gigi and I are heading to that window we're redecorating tonight. Taking these old alarm clocks over there now."

"Good. Oh, yeah. About that window. Gigi, make sure I get the money for those mannequins before they leave the store tonight." A cell phone rings, distracting the manager. "It's security. Now what?" he asks, stepping aside. "Yeah, Jameson? What is it?" The manager sighs. "You're joking. Well, see what you can find out."

The shiny black shoes follow Ray and Gigi over to their cart. "Seems Jameson, store security, heard from Barbara, over in cosmetics, about some girl models working the main floor. Heard anything about it?"

There is no response from Ray or Gigi. "Had a dog with them, too. Sounds fishy to me."

"It's news to us, boss. But we'll keep our eyes peeled. Ready, Gigi?" There is a squeak and the sound of footsteps as the cart slowly moves.

The nasal voice continues. "Well, you know what a talker Barbara is. Never stops, but the customers love her makeovers. Anyway, Jameson is on the case." There is a threatening chuckle before he calls back, "Oh, and Gigi, I'll be on your case if I don't get the money for those heads. Tonight."

Elise shakes so hard the surrounding greenery trembles. "Chillax!" Maxzyne mouths.

"Not to worry, Mr. Tracy," Gigi answers. "Got my heart set on those heads!"

The crouching girls breathe out, relieved, when the squeaky wheels moving Ray's cart grow faint and the shiny black shoes disappear, footsteps fading.

"Oh, I just hope no one notices I'm gone from the display," Elise groans.

"Well, not much we can do now." Maxzyne stands, stepping away from the screen. She turns to give Elise a hand up. "Besides, grown-ups don't notice much. They'll probably just drop their stuff off, get their paychecks, take a coffee break, whatever, and come back later. We've got to think positive! Oh, and Elise? You can stop squeezing my arm! It's real, remember?"

7

The Fourth Floor

"IT'S SO WEIRD. Mom and I were just here." Maxzyne steps onto the escalator. She cranes her neck to see Level Four from the Grand Hall. "Pretty soon I'm going to be old enough for juniors, though." She points to the sign for juniors department on Level Three.

Elise is more enchanted by the escalator. "It's like a moving staircase, isn't it?" she says. She holds the handrail tight as they are lifted higher into the lofty atrium. Maxzyne looks at her, surprised. Elise shrugs. "I've always been on the back elevator before. They cram us into the car along with the display furniture when the store is closed. Believe me, it's not open and fun like this. Sometimes we're not even dressed! Maman just hates that."

"Sorry. I keep forgetting you're not . . ." Maxzyne fades off uncertainly.

"Real? Well, for now I am. So I'm going to enjoy every minute!" Elise throws her arms out dramatically. They both giggle.

"Shhh!" Maxzyne puts a finger to her lips. "Better not attract any attention! Keep a lookout for Mr. Tracy or anyone from security."

Elise hangs over the black rubber handrail, waist bent, feet rising from the moving stair, hoping to get a better look. "No one in sight so far. Oops!"

Maxzyne jerks Elise back by the shoulders. "Watch out, Elise! Real girls can't fly!" She turns to look over the floor below. "You're right. No Tracy in sight."

Grinning, Elise lowers her heels back down onto the step. "You know, Ray says 'Mr. Tracy doesn't know crap about fashion or display.' Otherwise he wouldn't be getting rid of us." Falling silent, she looks thoughtful. They move toward the next set of stairs and continue their ascent.

"Elise!" Maxzyne pokes her companion's arm. "You can't say that."

"Say what?"

"Crap." Maxzyne shakes her head, looking grave. "We can't say it at school. Our language arts teacher, Ms. Clark, says there's always a better word than a bad word. And 'crap' is like, you know, poop." She makes a face. "And Mother would wash my mouth out with soap if I said it."

"Sorry! I didn't know." Elise looks worried. "What

else? Are there other things real girls shouldn't say? You better tell me!"

"Probably. My parents only let me watch G-rated stuff. They say 'it's for my own protection.' Protection from what? That's what I want to know!" She shakes her head, rolling her eyes. "It's so lame! Nothing but baby programs! My friends, Gayle and Erika, say I'm in the 'kid maximum security protection program.'"

Maxzyne rests one leg on the higher step, anticipating their arrival at the next level. Elise does the same. But she is distracted by a smudge on her white, patent leather shoe.

Maxzyne leans on the handrail. "I can't wait 'til I'm thirteen! I'll get to watch PG movies, have sleepovers, and be on the computer by myself! But 'til then, Mom says those are the rules."

Elise is still rubbing her shoe. She nearly trips on the flattening step.

Maxzyne grabs her arm. "Careful!"

"There are an awful lot of rules when you're a real girl, aren't there?" Elise worries. They step onto the next escalator, which is rising toward Level Four.

Maxzyne nods, sighing. Suddenly, her eyes twinkle mischievously. "Hey! It's just us right now. Who needs rules? It's our adventure, right?" She raises her fist toward Elise, who looks confused. "Here, make a fist like this." Taking Elise's hand, Maxzyne shows her how to curl her fingers tight. Then she bumps it lightly with her own fist. They bump fists several times, giggling. They nearly fall when the escalator dumps them off at the next level.

"We're here! Level Four!"

"Come on! Let's shop!"

Maxzyne makes a beeline for the nearest rack. She immediately starts looking through the striped shirts, cotton shorts, and matching pleated skirts.

Elise is more cautious. From behind a table stacked high with soft cardigans, she peers toward the service counter. She watches the clerk, a slender, older woman with silvery hair, fold a customer's purchase in white tissue paper.

"Maxzyne! Stay over here, so Ms. Mitchell won't see us."

"Okay, chillax already. So that's who Ray's got a crush on, huh?" Maxzyne giggles. She runs her hand along the hanging clothes, admiring the rippling waves of color. "It's kind of like a rainbow, don't you think?" She suddenly claps a hand over her mouth. Her eyes grow wide. "Sorry, Elise! I keep forgetting you're . . ."

"I did see a rainbow once." Elise gets a faraway look in her eyes. "I was in a display window on the State Street side, and the sun was shining. But then it started to rain." She looks over at Maxzyne, who is checking the size of a blue, pleated tennis skirt, before continuing. "Anyway, people stood in the doorway or huddled under the awning. Everyone was pointing and smiling. It was so beautiful."

"Hey! Check it out!" Maxzyne interrupts. She holds up a neon-green tennis dress. With her free hand, she pretends to swing a tennis racket.

"Serena Williams, ace wins the point!" Dropping her robe, she slides into the dress. She smoothes it down over her hips and swimsuit. "You know, if I wasn't already going to be an artist like Faith Livingston, my doll, I'd be a tennis star instead."

"Can you be whoever you want if you're a real girl?" Elise wonders aloud.

"Mother says once I'm grownup, I can be anything—as long as I do my homework and make good grades in school. It's just taking so long to grow up!"

"I guess if I could be anything, I'd be a writer," Elise offers. "I really like to make up stories about people."

"You do? Then you must have a big imagination, too. Same as me."

"I'm always telling Peppin stories about people I see walking by the window."

Maxzyne nods. "Hey! Did you make up a story about me?"

"I didn't have to. I heard you wishing for a polka-dot poodle like Peppin to play with. So did Esmeralda."

"Oh. Yeah."

"Anyway, I watch people all day. I don't know them, but I can make something up. Papa says that's what writers do."

"Sure. But you know that homeless woman, Esmeralda? You said she talks to you."

Elise nods.

Maxzyne's eyes narrow. "She's kind of creepy. Don't you think? I mean, it must make her a little weird, being homeless. Because if she only talks to, uh . . . windows."

"You mean she talks to mannequins. Like us." Elise raises her eyebrows. Maxzyne nods, shrugging uneasily. "Well, at least Esmeralda really sees us. I mean, every once in a while, someone might stop to look at the merchandise. But they don't really pay attention to us mannequins . . . not really." She stoops to pick up a fallen tag from the floor. "I think it's because real people are always in a hurry, aren't they?"

Maxzyne nods. "I know I am! Counting the days 'til I'm thirteen."

Elise wrinkles her brow, thinking. "I guess it's exciting to go places, meet new people, and do different things every day. But I can only imagine when I watch from the window."

"Well, I can't wait 'til I'm old enough to travel. I want to see the whole world. Africa! The Amazon! The South Pole!" Maxzyne throws her arms out wide.

"I don't know about the South Pole. But I'd like to take Maman and Papa to Paris! My favorite seamstress, Jacqueline, was from there."

Smiling, Elise does a little twirl. Then she points to Maxzyne's tennis dress. "We better get going. Is that what you're wearing to meet Gigi?"

"I don't know. You think she likes sports?" Maxzyne wanders over to another rack. "Or is this better?" She holds up a purple pants set with black trim and shiny silver buttons.

Elise frowns. "Hmmm. What do you really like? Gigi is an artist, and you want to be one someday, right?" Maxzyne nods. "So wouldn't you both like the same kind of clothes?"

"Are you kidding? She looks like a vampire!" Maxzyne returns the pants set to the rack. "But maybe that's because artists like to be different." She selects a ruffled pink skirt with filmy strips of white silk that come down to her knees. "Nope. Too over-the-top. That's what Mother would say. She always picks out my clothes." Demonstrating, Maxzyne rests her hand above her knee before sliding it several inches higher on her thigh. She chants, "Skirts to here. Shorts to there. Halter tops—don't you dare!" Her voice rises. "'Age-appropriate' is her favorite word!" she adds, scowling.

"Sounds like more of those real girl rules," Elise says. She follows Maxzyne around another circular rack. Forgetting to be careful, they wander dangerously close to the service counter. They draw back quickly.

"Hey! Look at this!"

Maxzyne grabs a denim skirt with ivory lace cut-outs along the knee-length hem. Elise finds a matching light blue T-shirt with puffy lace cut-outs in the sleeves. She holds it near the skirt. Maxzyne looks at the costume and frowns.

"It's too matchy-matchy," she pronounces, returning the shirt to the rack. "Not enough fashionation."

"Is that a word?"

"Is now. I just made it up! Fashion, imagination. Get it?"

Elise nods, holding the denim skirt. Glancing toward the sales clerk, she waves impatiently. "Come on. We better hurry. Ms. Mitchell is finished with that customer."

"Hey, look! This is perfect! What do you think?" Maxzyne yanks a denim jacket with colorful stick figures from the rack. "This is exactly what I'd wear!" she exclaims. "And look over here!" She runs to a shoe display across the aisle. "How about these?" she asks, grabbing a pair of red suede boots. "Cool, huh?" She checks the size. "Yeah, they'll fit."

Maxzyne peels off the tennis dress. She throws it to Elise who catches it in midair and tosses back the denim skirt. Maxzyne quickly shrugs the jacket over her shoulders and pulls on the boots. Pulling her hair out of her face, she rushes to admire her new look in the closest full-length mirror.

"Awesome, right?"

Elise nods approvingly. She conscientiously returns the tennis dress to its proper hanger and rack.

"All you need is one of those artist's berets. Papa and I wore them in a Picasso window display once."

"Picasso?" Maxzyne smiles. "Now, that's definitely cool. And I like the hat idea. Weren't hats over this way?" Maxzyne wanders in the direction of the checkout counter. Seconds later, she stops short. This causes Elise to bump into her from behind. Ahead, Ms. Mitchell quietly tags clothes. Her back is to them.

Fingers to lips, the two girls slip between a table display of socks and lacy tights and leggings. They arrive at the hat display in the far corner. Then they pause, taking a quick glance toward the service counter.

"Wait! Where'd she go?" Maxzyne whispers.

"Maybe to the back." Elise worriedly looks over the department. "Sometimes a new shipment comes in, and they have to do inventory. Hurry! Pick a hat before she comes back out!"

Maxzyne spins the revolving hat rack. She skims over white bonnets with ribbons and pansies, straw hats with sunflowers, paisley, soft-brimmed newsboy hats, slouchy denim sun hats, neon visors, and baseball caps with "Cubs" and "Sox" logos.

"My dad took me to a Cubs game once," she recalls. She tries on a cap and faces the brim backwards. "They had great corn dogs!"

"Just hurry, Maxzyne!"

"Okay, okay. Here's one. What do you think?" Maxzyne tucks her braids into a woven, brimless, round hat with a flat crown. She wrinkles her nose at the round mirror. "Nope, this is *so* not me."

Caught up in the search, Elise giggles. She reaches for a navy scout cap. She carefully tucks her blonde ponytail inside, shaking her head and mimicking Maxzyne. "This is *so* not me!"

Maxzyne ignores Elise and tries on a white sailor hat. She salutes her own reflection in the mirror. "Well, this would go with my swimsuit. But it's really not 'artsy,' is it?" She shakes her head. She spins the display, spies a black, flat cap with a small brim, and puts it on. "Elise, I think I—"

From the other side of the hat rack, Elise plucks a safari helmet from a high hook. She arranges it over her ponytail and secures the elastic band under her chin. Then she leans forward, and Maxzyne laughs out loud.

"Elise, you look like *Animal Apprentice!*" she shrieks. Then she immediately claps her hand over her mouth. Together, they drop to the floor. They scurry under a rack of clothes in a muffled fit of giggles.

"What do you mean?" Elise whispers. "Real animals don't wear hats, do they?"

"Duh! It's a cool TV show where kids learn about wildlife," Maxzyne whispers back. "It's like . . . they track lions, wrestle giant snakes in Africa, stuff like that. Someone's always wearing one of those hats and swatting mosquitoes."

Turning serious, Maxzyne rises to peer over the top of a headband display. "Do you think she heard us?"

There is no sign of Ms. Mitchell. Elise joins Maxzyne, and their eyes travel the length of the girls' department. They are still alone.

"Whew! We've got to get going," Maxzyne urges. She adjusts the cap so that it dips below one ear. "This outfit looks cool enough for Gigi. Don't you think?"

"Positively. And when we get back downstairs, let's find a shawl for Maman, too."

"Oh, yeah. For her goose bumps."

"Why do they call them goose bumps, Maxzyne?"

Maxzyne concentrates on her image in the mirror. She moves several braids forward from under the hat. They fall against her smooth cheek. "I think it's because when the goose is plucked it—"

From above, a grasping arm suddenly appears. It grabs Maxzyne by the shoulder. "Your goose is cooked, girls. Caught red-handed," accuses a booming, male voice.

With a shriek, Maxzyne ducks. She wriggles frantically out of the man's grasp, making a getaway somersault away from the gray-cuffed pants and black, thick-soled police shoes. Scrambling beneath a clothes rack, she watches the clunky feet temporarily moving in the wrong direction. "Over here, Elise," she hisses. The man, who must be store security, angrily rifles the clothes rack above Elise. She is cowering below, as yet unnoticed. "Quick!"

Elise runs over to the rack of Easter dresses, making pastels swing on their white, plastic hangers. On all fours, the girls scamper toward the escalator. Soft, gray carpet muffles their escape.

"Get back here, you! You were right. There's two of 'em. Ms. Mitchell, they're going that way. Head them off!"

"Oh! You terrible girls! Where are your mothers?" The elderly woman cannot bend far enough over to see beneath the racks. She rushes from one clothes carousel to another, peering between hangers. "I'm sorry, Mr. Jameson. My knees aren't what they used to be. I don't see them!"

Elise and Maxzyne watch from beneath a rack of sale coats near the escalator. Moving cautiously out from under the winter sales goods, they edge toward the escalator. Behind them, Jameson grunts. He thrashes and paws his way through the hanging clothes.

"I guess it's a good thing I called you, Mr. Jameson. They thought I didn't see them fooling around. But they made me suspicious."

"We'll find them!" Jameson answers. "Won't get far, ma'am. Store's locked tight as a drum in a few minutes."

"I better make sure my cash register is locked."

Jameson straightens up with a low moan. "Ouch, my back! Come out, right now, you two! Give up! It's only going to be worse for you, if you don't!"

Ms. Mitchell's voice grows close again. "It's a scandal, you know. All these years working in the girls' department, and I've never seen shoplifters this young. Stealing! Is the economy really as bad as that? Where are their parents? Why, in my day, we were always accompanied by an adult."

"These days, ma'am, kids are into everything. Shoplifting, petty crime, drugs, you name it. Parents don't pay attention to their kids! Well, I've got a nose for shoplifters. So don't you worry! And maybe," he adds, lowering his voice, "I'll even get that promotion after I catch them."

"Well, I hope you won't be too hard on them." Ms. Mitchell's voice is softer. "They looked terribly young!"

"If you ask me, we should turn them over to the cops and throw the book at them. Big fine, lock 'em up in juvenile detention. That'll teach 'em!"

Out in the open and inching toward the escalator, the girls hold their breath. Maxzyne reaches the metal platform first. She pulls Elise with her, bracing one leg against the railing to keep from falling. Afraid to look up, the two carefully crawl backwards onto the steps. Then they rise, turn, and run quickly down the moving stairs. At the third floor landing, they stop to take a quick look back.

"Let's just get to the lower level," Elise pants. "I know more places to hide and other stairs we can use if we need to run."

"Okay," Maxzyne agrees. "But first let's find a ladies' room. Better wash my hands and straighten up before I meet Gigi. Look."

"Oh, yuk." Elise wrinkles her nose at Maxzyne's stained palms. Raising her own hands, she is shocked to see they are dirty. "From the escalator steps?"

Maxzyne nods. "Where to, Elise? Lead the way."

Elise points to the right, in the direction of the electronics department. "I think it's that way. Follow me."

The two girls race off. They spot the "Ladies Room" sign just as a musical chime is heard over the store loudspeaker.

"Attention, Crowne's customers. Our store is now closing. We will reopen again tomorrow at 10:00 a.m. Please proceed to the nearest checkout counter with your purchases, and thank you for shopping at Crowne's Emporium."

"Hey, Elise?" The other girl does not turn around. Instead, she darts into an opening leading toward a large door with a brass handle.

"What, Maxzyne?" The heavy door creaks on its hinges as the two girls enter.

"No way that security guy finds us in the Ladies Room, huh?"

8

The Ladies' Room

SOAP BUBBLES FLY as Maxzyne scrubs her hands at one of the white sinks standing in a row. Above the sinks, a gleaming mirror runs the length of the back wall of the large room. There are two soft couches and several chairs near the far wall, but luckily the girls have the place to themselves. Admiring her reflection, Maxzyne flicks water from her fingertips and straightens her hat. "Hey! What are you doing, Elise?"

Standing at the next sink, Elise is spellbound by the soap dispenser. She moves her hand close and then pulls it away. Slowly, she moves her hand back, as if she were trying to sneak up on the little machine. "Oh!" A puffy cloud of soap squirts into her waiting, dirt-streaked palm. "Is it alive, Maxzyne? How does it know?" She bends to inspect the dispenser, searching for the eye that must surely be watching.

This movement causes another cloud of foam to be released, catching her by surprise when it lands softly on her forehead. Perplexed, she wipes it away with the back of her hand.

"Of course it's not alive," Maxzyne laughs. "It's just . . . well, I don't know, programmed or something. If you move, it moves. Like the automatic flush toilets back there," she adds, pointing toward the long row of stalls in the adjoining room. "Come here," she says. When Elise looks confused, Maxzyne walks to the nearest stall and steps halfway in to prove her point.

Both girls jump at the sudden noise of the flushing toilet. "Wow! See what I mean? It knows you're there!" Elise looks alarmed.

Maxzyne gives a little cackle. "And this towel dispenser does, too. Watch out!" She skips over to the wall-mounted paper towel dispenser, waving her hand beneath it. With a mechanical hum, it dispenses ten inches of white paper. She rips off the waiting paper towel and quickly dries her hands. Glancing around, she confidently tosses the damp ball toward the bin across the room. It lands inside.

"Score!" Raising her arms triumphantly, Maxzyne grins at Elise. "Three points from outside the paint!"

"Shhhh. They'll hear us in here, Maxzyne!" Back at the sink, Elise brings the soapy foam to her nose, sniffing curiously. Rubbing her hands together, she is fascinated as the foam turns brown from the grime on her hands. As she scrubs, she says, "Real people are so strange. They can do anything, but they have automatic machines to do everything for them, don't they?"

"Sure, why not? Engineers invent stuff and it makes life easier and faster, I guess. Hey, are you done playing with the soap? We've got to get you back to the window like I promised Mr., er, your father."

Elise nods, quickly rinsing her hands and stepping to the towel dispenser. Holding up her hands, she waits, grinning when the paper curls out toward her fingers. Ripping it awkwardly across the metal teeth, she carefully dries her hands and then inspects her palms for any missed dirt.

Suddenly, they hear voices approaching from the outside passageway. Behind them, the door groans, beginning to open. Both girls freeze, listening.

"Good evening to you, Ms. Mitchell," says a familiar voice.

"Oh no, it's that cosmetics lady! Quick! In here." Maxzyne jerks open a door marked "Utility Storage," pulling Elise by the arm. The closet is dark and stuffy and smells like cleansers, but there's just enough space to hide beneath the bottom shelf if they crouch behind the brooms and mops. Luckily, a screen near the top of the door allows some light to shine through and a bit of fresh air to get in.

"Why, Ms. Mitchell!" exclaims Barbara. "Heavens!

Is something wrong? You look a little . . . well, pale, if you don't mind my saying so. You should come visit my counter for a little Glam Diva Maquillage color! Our new spring palette, featuring Blossom, would look so, so, so, divine on you! You know, a little makeup—"

"Yes, I suppose I am looking a bit worn, dear. I've had quite a day—one of the worst ever!" There's a slight hiss. "Oh, that's better. I'll just sit for a minute. Anyway, we caught two girls stealing from my department. Girls' clothing! Can you believe it? I just don't understand society today, Barbara. They were just kids! I'm still upset about it. I called security, but even Mr. Jameson wasn't able to find them—just made a mess of the dress racks. I've really worn myself out trying to straighten up. Now I'll have to work late tonight. Thought I'd rest for a few minutes and catch my breath. This Ladies' Room is the only one with such comfy chairs."

"I know just what you mean about kid shoplifters—we have to watch them like hawks in cosmetics, too," the voice drifts from a distance. "Lip gloss, especially! But I don't mind calling on Jameson for a little law and order—he's kind of cute, don't you think so?"

"I hadn't really noticed, dear. I suppose."

"You wouldn't know if he's got a girlfriend by any chance, would you?" There's a distant whoosh as a toilet flushes. The voice gets closer again, and there's the sound of running water. "I never see him with anyone, but these days, you can never be sure, can you?"

Barbara's question is interrupted by another squeak of the door. Elise breathes in sharply. In the dark, Maxzyne gives her a warning poke in the arm.

"Hey, Ms. Mitchell!"

Gigi! Maxzyne clamps a hand over her own mouth, holding back a desperate urge to scream, burst through the door, and run for her life. *Just get me out of here!* She can see the whites of Elise's eyes. They reach for each other's hands and squeeze.

"And Barbara, too. What's up, ladies? Sounds like a little retail romance to me." Gigi's voice rises. "Oh, look at me! Forsythia pollen everywhere. This stuff sticks!"

"Here, let me help you, dear. It's all over your back." There is a hiss as Miss Mitchell rises. Seconds later, they hear the whir of the towel dispenser and then running water. "It's coming off, dear. Don't worry."

"You know, Ms. Mitchell, those pearls you're wearing remind me of our new finishing powder, Pearlesse," Barbara calls from the adjoining room. "Stop by, and I'll give you a sample."

"Still looking to find a man to try out some of your free samples on, Barbara?" Gigi gives a little snort.

Barbara's retort is good-natured. "Any and all ideas welcome! I was just saying that Jameson's kind of my type: big, strong, and manly—"

"You must be talking about his hands, not his brain!"

"Gigi!" Ms. Mitchell's voice crackles across the room. "That's downright mean."

"Sorry! Guess all that pollen's gone to my brain." She sighs. "Ray and I have several hours to work, yet. I don't know how he stays so calm—especially when Tracy is always on his case! Me? I'm ready to use a blow torch on him!"

"Well . . ." The elderly woman hesitates. "I think Ray knows enough about Mr. Tracy to have patience with his bad moods."

"Really?" Barbara chirps. "Oooh! Do tell. How do

you know?"

"Well, his wife, of course. She was in my department, buying a dress for her niece a while ago. It was the sweetest smocked dress with—"

"Never mind that," Barbara interrupts. "Give us the dirt on Tracy."

"It's not dirt, Barbara. It's just sad. Years ago, Mr. Tracy and his wife were in a car accident. She was pregnant, and they lost the baby. She could never have another one, although they tried. Poor lady. The only time I ever saw her smile was when she talked about her niece. And her doll collection. It sounded quite extensive. Can you imagine?"

"Wow," says Gigi. "Who knew? That explains a lot."

"Tragic. Just tragic!" Barbara clucks. Her heels tip-tap toward the door. "I'll tell you what else is tragic—these poor feet of mine! Luckily, I'll be sitting down to finish my sales figures. Well, better not keep Mr. Tracy waiting. He lives for the numbers. Bye, ladies." The door hinges squeak.

"Please don't repeat what I told you, Barbara," warns Ms. Mitchell. "I'm sure Mr. Tracy doesn't want everyone to know his private business."

"My lips are sealed. Lip liner does that too, you know!" She giggles as the door creaks closed behind her.

Trapped too long in an awkward crouch, Maxzyne's foot suddenly cramps. "Owwww!" she moans. She shifts her position and knocks over a broom. She is horrified when the wooden handle thuds against the closet.

"What was that?" Gigi asks sharply.

Silence. Maxzyne covers her face, afraid to breathe. Beside her, Elise trembles.

"Old pipes. Maybe a ghost," Ms. Mitchell answers. "This building must be filled with ghosts after all these years."

Gigi gives a snort. "Yeah. A dead shopper just realized his sales coupon expired!" She laughs, opening the door.

"Goodness, Gigi. Have respect for the spirits!" Ms. Mitchell's kindly voice grows fainter as the two women exit.

"You know, Ray's got a few ghost stories about this place. You two could compare them and. . . ." The heavy door groans shut.

Seconds later, Maxzyne and Elise creep from the closet.

"Yikes! I thought they'd never go! Ugh! It was stuffy in there. And that smell! Like bleach or something." Looking in the mirror, Maxzyne wrinkles her nose, automatically straightening her hat.

"Let's just *go*, Maxzyne!" Elise pulls on the heavy door, and it groans once more. She looks nervous. "Have you ever seen a ghost, Maxzyne? I remember Cecile, the head seamstress, used to tell stories about ghosts when she was doing fittings late at night. How the ghosts would haunt people and drive them crazy and—"

"The only thing haunting us is Jameson, that security guy. Let's go! We are *so* out of here!"

9

Making Music

A S THEY EXIT THE ladies' room on Level Three, Maxzyne pauses in the hallway and looks carefully around the floor. "Okay, the coast is clear. What's the best way back to the window?"

"Right behind you," Elise replies. She points toward the far end of the electronics department. "There's an old stairway over there."

"Good idea!" The girls stride in that direction. "Elise, Jameson won't give up, will he?"

"Not Jameson. He's always looking to catch shoplifters. I think he wants a promotion or something." Elise suddenly giggles.

"What's so funny?"

"Jameson. He's still pretty new on the job," answers Elise. "Just last week, he got in big trouble. Mr. Tracy's wife bought a new dress. She liked it so much she wanted to wear it that minute. Well, the clerk forgot to remove the security tag. So when Mrs. Tracy left the store by the door nearest our window, the alarms went off. She didn't even know it was her dress causing all the uproar. But Jameson ran out and grabbed her. He didn't recognize her, so he called the police. Pretty soon, Mr. Tracy showed up and yelled at Jameson in front of everyone. So Jameson's probably trying to get back in his good graces. No wonder he's on the lookout for real shoplifters."

"Well, let's stay off his radar, huh?" Maxzyne leads the way through the electronics department. She darts behind columns and creeps past blinking displays of devices. Then Maxzyne slows, looking worried. "I guess my mother's radar is going full speed right now, wondering where I am." She looks back at the escalators. The lights have dimmed for closing. They are casting long shadows everywhere. "It's getting late. I was supposed to set the table and pack my suitcase while she took a nap." She swallows hard. "Because I gave her a headache. She's going to kill me when she finds out I sneaked out of the condo." For emphasis, she draws a line across her throat. Then, for good measure, she rolls her eyes and sticks out her tongue, making a gagging sound.

Elise gasps, eyes wide. "Kill you?" she gulps. "Really?"

"Well, uh, no . . . 'course not! I'm just being a drama queen."

"A what?"

"I'm being dramatic!" Maxzyne tosses her braids away from her face.

Oh!" Elise sighs, looking relieved. "Thank goodness. You scared me."

"But I'll be grounded for the rest of my life. At least."

"Grounded? Like being cooped up in a window all your life?"

"Well, when you put it that way . . ." Shamefaced, Maxzyne nods. "Yeah. Sort of."

"But you're helping us! She'll understand. Won't she? When you tell her about us? She just has to!"

Maxzyne shakes her head. "Probably not. She'll say I made it all up. I do that a lot, I guess. She says I have an overactive imagination."

"But maybe that's a good thing," Elise says. "I mean, Esmeralda must have noticed your imagination and known you were just the one to save us. Right?"

"Yeah, but this is something even I never imagined."

"Look! Almost to the staircase." Elise points across the carpeted expanse of the young men's department. "We can sneak down those old stairs. Nobody will know, as long as we're really quiet."

Maxzyne doesn't watch where she's walking. Her hip catches on the corner of a computerized musical instrument display. The table wobbles sharply. Both girls watch, horrified, as the entire exhibit shakes and falls apart.

"Look out!" Maxzyne hisses. She barely catches a guitar before it hits her in the head.

Elise gives a little shriek. She dives low, and a keyboard falls into her arms. Her helmet is knocked sideways on her head. Clutching the keyboard to her chest, she cradles the black and white keys as if her life depended on it. She kneels, shaking her head at Maxzyne.

"Wow! That was close, Elise." Maxzyne steadies the table as pamphlets flutter to the floor around her. "Good save!" She sits down cross-legged beside Elise, holding the electronic guitar. "Wait, I've heard of this!" she exclaims. "Be Your Own Band," she reads from a fallen brochure. "One of the kids in my class has this! He says it's super cool and . . . oooh, we've got to try it." She jumps to her feet, holding the guitar. Its black cord dangles. "Where's the closest outlet?"

"We can't, Maxzyne!" Elise protests. "Are you crazy? Jameson or one of the night staff will hear us!"

"Not if we plug this in . . ."

Holding the silver guitar plug, Maxzyne searches under the display. "Just as I thought. Here's one," she announces, her voice muffled. "Now grab yours."

Elise unwillingly hands her the black keyboard cord. "I don't see how this is going to work. We really should be—"

"You don't see it, you hear it!" Maxzyne squeals. She removes the helmet from Elise's head and replaces it with a set of headphones. Then she grabs a pair for herself.

"Okay, ready for action? Soon as I find the 'on' switch, which is . . . right . . . here!" Standing, she pushes several buttons on the shiny, blue guitar. She grins when small red dots flash on the neck. "That's it! C'mon, Elise, get ready to rock!"

"But I don't know how to—"

"Doesn't matter," Maxzyne interrupts. "It's all programmed. Whatever we play, the computer turns into music." She points her guitar neck at the display sign. "C'mon. Let's be our own band!"

Elise looks unconvinced. "But shouldn't we be—"

"Elise! You're the one who said you wanted to make the most of every minute being real, didn't you? Well, here's your chance. Be real for once!"

Elise moves her fingers over the keys. Her eyes widen in surprise. She pauses and then tries again, more confidently.

Listening through her own headphones, Maxzyne nods. She taps her foot to Elise's strengthening beat. Finally, she leans over and gives her an approving fist bump.

"My turn." Maxzyne bounces on her toes. She is dying to try the guitar. "Watch this." She pulls the strap over her shoulder, adjusts the instrument on her hip, and pretends to be a rock star. Raising her chin, legs slightly bent at the knees, she closes her eyes and puts her fingers over the guitar neck. Maxzyne instantly feels famous. Eyes closed and heart racing, she imagines an adoring crowd clapping and chanting her name.

"Maxzyne!"

"Maxzyne!"

"Maxzyne!"

Guitar and piano chords crash and explode inside their ears. The girls take turns, heads bobbing and feet tapping together. They are spellbound. Several braids escape from under Maxzyne's cap. Her sparkling

barrettes flash, rising and falling with the frenzied motion of her hands. Growing bolder, she moves wildly to the beat, kicking her legs in the air. She closes her eyes and hears her fans whistle and scream her name. "Maxzyne!" She jumps again, this time higher. But a blinding flash and loud Pzzzzzzzzz-zzzt return her to the real world.

Her guitar shakes. What's happening? Her eyes follow the dark cord where it dangles uselessly. It has been ripped in half by her wild jumping. Uh oh. No wonder the smell of burnt plastic rises from the carpet where tendrils of smoke are beginning to curl from the broken cord. Yikes! Fire! Maxzyne yanks the long end of the cord out of the wall. She is relieved to see there are no sparks.

Frightened, Elise leaps backward, nostrils flaring. The entire floor goes dark. Seconds later, they hear a faint beeping sound coming from somewhere near the elevators. Here and there, dim emergency lights flash on. But the store around them remains quite dark.

"Uh oh, I think we blew a circuit!" Maxzyne gasps. She wriggles out of the guitar strap. She leaves the shiny, blue instrument on the tile floor and pulls Elise to her feet. "C'mon! We've got to get out of here before we're caught!"

Making no attempt to be quiet, they flee. Alarm clocks, radios, and assorted small electronics fall from carefully stacked shelves and tables as they stumble around in near darkness.

"Wait! Slow down," Elise warns, stopping. "The stairs are right there."

Maxzyne skids to a stop. "Shhhhh. Did you hear that?" she whispers in Elise's ear. "Listen."

At the top of the stairs, they pause. There is the faint sound of men talking. It is interrupted by radio static coming from the far side of the electronics department. The sudden glow of a flashlight pierces the dark. It bounces off the ceiling. They watch as it skitters over a nearby column, nearly catching them in its glare. The next time the ray of light sweeps toward them, the girls duck. Then they begin to creep quietly down the stairs.

"Are you sure you know where we're going, Elise?"

"Straight to the lower level. All the way down to where that—"

"Are you serious? That's where the Lollipop and Soda Shop is! I *thought* I smelled chocolate! I'm totally starving!" Without waiting for an answer, Maxzyne rushes down the stairwell. She quickly disappears.

"Maxzyne!" Elise whispers. "Maxzyne! Wait! I can't see you!! Slow down!" There is no response. Groaning in frustration, she lets go of the handrail. She impatiently whips her long hair out of her eyes and slips off her white Mary Janes. Holding a shoe in each hand, Elise rushes down the stairs as fast as she dares, following Maxzyne in the dark.

10

Birthday Wishes

"AWESOME! LOOK! It's everything Easter!" Jumping down the last three steps, Maxzyne slides to a stop on the colored tiles of the Lollipop and Soda Shop. It's a sugary wonderland: rows and shelves of candy jars, an old fashioned soda fountain, and tempting displays of boxed chocolates and other sweet treats. "C'mon, Elise. You're going to love this place." Skipping up to the polished wooden counter, she trails her fingers along oversized glass jars of candies lined up like soldiers on parade. Pausing, she considers a container of butter cream mints. The pale green and white nougats make her mouth water. Lifting the lid, she grins as the scent of peppermint, vanilla, and sugar rises in the air. She snatches a candy from inside the jar and drops it in her mouth, letting it float on her tongue. The sugar rush makes her giddy, and she quickly moves on. To her right is a bouquet of sweet and sour lollipops with colorful swirls. Selecting two lollipops from their ceramic pots, she teases Elise by holding them up to her eyes. Sticking out a minty tongue, she gurgles, "Look! Lollipop eyes!" Laughing at her own silliness, she moves on to another jar.

A disapproving frown on her face, Elise stands on the last step, arms crossed, refusing to join in.

Maxzyne doesn't notice. She is already charmed by a platter of glossy chocolate Easter bunnies wearing white top hats with lilac bands and collars trimmed in pink roses. "Just one—we'll share," she says, picking up a small, woven basket. She carefully chooses one of the mouth-watering bunnies and places it inside. Still not content, she stoops to admire the chocolate truffles displayed on delicate paper doilies lining silver platters inside a gleaming display case.

"Oh, wow! I've got to be dreaming!" Maxzyne's nose smudges the glass as she reads the labels. "Chocolate Trifle . . . Peanut Surprise . . . Coco-Delite . . . Caramel Crunch . . . Strawberry Cream . . . Deviled Chocolate—yummmmmm! Hey, Elise, what do you want?"

Her lips pressed in a thin line, Elise doesn't answer.

Maxzyne turns around, impatient at Elise's delay. She is shocked to see her standing next to the stairs. Pointing to the red-and-white striped stools by the soda fountain, she motions for Elise to join her. "C'mon! What are you waiting for? Let's eat—last one to their seat's a rotten Easter egg!" she declares, running to the nearest stool. With a triumphant squeal, she sits down and twirls back and forth on it.

Elise refuses to budge. "I'm not a rotten Easter egg!" Her frown deepening, she stamps her foot. "And you can't push me around just because you're a real girl!"

"Say what?"

"You just called me a rotten egg!"

"But I didn't mean, uh, I mean, that's just what kids say, Elise. You know, when you're racing someone, that's all. It's nothing personal." Her voice rises with indignation. "Besides, what do you mean I'm pushing you around? I'm trying to save you, remember?"

"Save me?" Elise's shoulders quiver. She takes a shaky breath, hands on her hips. "We were nearly caught because you had to have a hat. Then we almost started a fire because you had to play music. Now you're eating candy!" she accuses, her voice growing shrill. She glares across the room at Maxzyne.

"What's up? You didn't seem to mind before. Thought we agreed it was no rules for real girls time, Elise."

Elise squares her shoulders, standing taller. "You still haven't convinced Gigi not to . . ." She swallows hard before continuing. "You know what? Just leave us alone. You're no help. You keep wasting time. Come to think of it, maybe you're just scared!"

"Scared? I am not!" Shocked, Maxzyne stops twirling in her chair. "Besides, we both decided I needed this hat, remember? And who's wasting time? Don't know about you, Elise, but real girls have to eat! I'm starved and I'm not going anywhere 'til I do!" To prove her point, she bites the top hat off a chocolate bunny.

Elise steps closer, changing tack. "But I have to get back to the window before I'm missed. And Maman and Papa will be worried if I'm not back!" she pleads. "Nooowwwww!"

Maxzyne quickly drops two jelly beans into Elise's gaping mouth. "Gotcha!" she squeals, dancing away from the other girl.

Nearly choking, Elise closes her mouth. Seconds later, her eyes light up as she chews, the gooey jelly bean center oozing over her tongue. Such delicious sweetness makes her shiver. "Okay, how long will this take?" she asks, reaching for another. Maxzyne smirks.

"Just long enough for us to sit down and try something else," Maxzyne answers, waving her arms at her version of paradise. Alone with all this candy and ice cream! A once in a lifetime opportunity. "Hey!" She grabs Elise's arm, pulling her toward another display. "Did you see these cupcakes?"

Now Elise is hooked. Within the twinkling lights decorating the graceful branches of a pink dogwood tree hang white china dessert plates edged in gold.

Each plate holds a heavily frosted, artfully decorated cupcake. Stepping close for a better look, she smells the creamy sweetness of vanilla and sugar. She can't help licking her lips. "Mmmm," she sighs.

Maxzyne grins, pleased with herself. After all, who doesn't like cupcakes?

"You know, Maxzyne," Elise recalls. "I was in a display here once, a long time ago. With Peppin. It was when the Crowne chocolate ladies first opened this cafe. But I never understood why the children were so happy and excited and, well, crazy over these treats! I thought it was just because they were with friends, celebrating their birthdays."

"Mother always gets three cupcakes to celebrate my birthday," Maxzyne tells her. "A red velvet for Dad, pineapple hummingbird for her, and double Dutch coco puff for me. Instead of one big cake, she says, everyone gets something they like and just the right amount." Making a face, she breathes in, sucking in her stomach and cheeks. "Can you tell she's always on a diet?"

Elise laughs. "Mannequins are *always* on a diet." She surveys the decorated cupcakes, standing tall in their tuxedo paper liners despite towering clouds of swirled icing. "I've never had a birthday," she admits. "What's it like, Maxzyne?"

"Birthdays?" Maxzyne looks stunned. Licking melted chocolate from her fingers, she frowns, wondering how to answer such a strange question. "Well, pretty much the best day in the whole world, I guess!" She laughs. "I'd say birthdays are even better than Christmas!"

"But why?" Elise brings her nose close enough to sniff a fluffy, pink strawberry cream cupcake. It is hanging exactly at eye level, perfectly balanced on a golden plate.

"That's easy! Because it's all about you, silly!" She twirls in her seat at the counter. "It's like, well, instead of Wednesday, the day is, you know, Maxzyne-day. From the time Mother wakes me up singing, 'til I go to bed that night, it's everything *me*."

"Oh, that sounds wonderful," Elise sighs. "So on that day, everyone thinks you're special. I'd like that." She moves on to a Coconut Cream Puff cupcake hanging nearby. The toasted coconut sprinkles fascinate her.

"Oh, you're special, all right. And the best part? You get presents!" Maxzyne jumps up and down, tugging at the necklace around her neck and making the tiny gold bell tinkle merrily. "Like this! And I got lots of other stuff, too."

"Do you feel any different when you're another year older on your birthday?"

Maxzyne looks puzzled. "Well, I . . . uh . . ." She pauses, thinking for a minute.

Not waiting for an answer, Elise finally reaches for

a banana split cupcake. Its golden cake body is covered in strawberry and chocolate swirls. A fat cherry tipped in chocolate crowns the glossy icing.

"Okay, not exactly." Maxzyne climbs back on the high stool. "I mean, it's not like you wake up and you're taller, you know. Smarter? . . . No. I guess . . . it's kind of something that just happens. You might not even notice, but it's your birthday and you're a little more grown-up. But you're still a kid!"

Elise carefully carries the cupcake to the counter, her eyes glittering.

"Hey! Know what?" Maxzyne leaps off the chair. "I've got an idea!"

"Not again." Elise rolls her eyes, climbing to sit on the high stool beside Maxzyne. "Last time you had an idea the lights went out."

"Nothing like that, Elise." Maxzyne claps her hands. "We're going to have a birthday party! Right now—for you!" She jumps down from her stool.

"Are you sure we can? How?"

"Like this. Watch." Maxzyne searches through the ceramic containers on the counter. "Don't eat that, yet!" she orders, pointing at Elise's cupcake.

With a sigh, Elise drops her fork.

Maxzyne spots a small cardboard box of striped birthday candles on the counter beside the napkins. Each slender, wax column is actually a number. "You're ten, right?"

"Yes, I'm supposed to be." Elise raises ten fingers. "That's what Maman has always told me. Why?"

"Let's say today's your birthday . . . that makes you . . ." Pausing dramatically, Maxzyne dumps the candles onto the counter. She picks out two, each shaped in the form of a number one. "Eleven!" She carefully stands one candle on each side of the fat cherry, squishing them down into the chocolate and strawberry frosting.

Elise touches the blue and white candles. "Eleven." She pauses. "I am? How can I be? I don't feel any different."

"Hey, we're not done yet. It's a party, remember? Now it's time to sing." Maxzyne steps back and takes a deep breath before suddenly exhaling in a rush.

"Wait! I forgot something big!" She rummages around on the counter among the containers and finally pounces on a small box of matches by the cash register. "Found them!"

Amazed, Elise watches Maxzyne strike the red match tip against the scratchy side of the box several times. "C'mon!" she urges, trying again. At last, the red tip hisses and then flares into a bright flame.

Elise jumps back, her nose wrinkling at the smell. "Fire! Oh, Maxzyne, you shouldn't do that! It's not safe!"

"It's okay. Mother lets me light candles all the time at home." Maxzyne touches the match to each candle and then steps away. "See? I'm experienced." She blows out the small flame with a flourish.

"It's so beautiful!" Elise admires the effect for a moment. Then she reaches for her plastic fork. "Can I eat it now?"

"No, not yet!" Maxzyne puts her hand in front of the cupcake. "I still have to sing!"

"Oh. All right." Elise sets the fork down again. Maxzyne stands tall and breathes in dramatically, throwing her arms out wide. Smiling, she sings in a high, sweet voice.

Hooray, it's your day.
May good things come your way.
One wish and a candle
To mark your new age.
May you be happy.
Today it's your stage!

Elise beams, clapping with delight. "Thank you, Maxzyne. That was perfect." She picks up the plastic fork, eager to taste her cupcake.

"No, stop!" Maxzyne shrieks.

"What now? It's *my* birthday!" Elise waves her fork impatiently.

"You still have to make a birthday wish," Maxzyne insists, pointing at the candles.

Elise looks confused. "A wish? Why?"

"Elise!" Maxzyne rolls her eyes, both hands on her hips. "Because it's your special day, that's why. On your birthday, you get one wish. It's like a little bit of magic just for you. Make a wish, then blow out the candles, and if you're lucky, it'll come true."

"But I'm not sure what to wish for." Elise looks worried. "What do you wish for on your birthday?"

Maxzyne thinks hard, chewing the inside of her cheek. "Well, I used to wish I had a sister. But that never happened. Now I wish my dad didn't have to work so much because he's never home, so it's just Mother, me, and her headaches. It would be so fun to have a . . ." She looks down, her voice trailing off.

Elise beams. "I know what to wish for!" She closes her eyes. "I wish I—"

Maxzyne jerks forward, covering Elise's mouth with her hand. The startled girl's eyes fly open in shock.

"No! You can't say it out loud, Elise. It's a secret wish just for you. Otherwise it might not come true." Maxzyne takes her hand away from Elise's mouth. "Okay?"

"But you just told me yours!" Elise protests.

"But it's not my birthday!"

The two girls stare solemnly at the candles flickering on the cupcake. Puddles of slowly melting frosting form around their edges.

"Ready? Close your eyes and wish as hard as you can." Hands resting in her lap, Elise solemnly obeys.

"I've done it," Elise announces. Her blue eyes shine.

"Can I blow the candles out now, and see if it comes true?"

"Yeah, go ahead. Blow hard!"

Taking the deepest breath, Elise leans toward the candles. Her face turns pink. Her lips form a perfect "O" as she blows. The candles sputter and go out. Flecks of melting blue wax are sprayed on the counter.

"Wow! Great job!" Maxzyne claps, jumping up and down.

Blushing with pride, Elise picks up her fork.

"Now we'll have to see if your wish comes true."

"I think it will," she answers confidently. Sticking her fork into the creamy icing, she brings it to her mouth, taking her first dainty bite. "But I still don't feel any different!" She glares at Maxzyne, who slyly dips her finger into a swirl of her cupcake frosting.

Licking her finger, Maxzyne smacks her lips. "Sharing is caring."

Elise moves the plate close and takes a bigger bite of cake.

"You know, maybe birthdays are special not because you're different but because other people think you're different," Maxzyne offers. "Now that you're eleven, something's changed, right?"

Crumbs fall from her chin as Elise nods, taking another forkful of cake. She opens her mouth wide and stuffs it in, declaring, "Now I'm older than you."

"Gross, Elise! You're spitting cake at me. And

anyway, you're just four months older. My birthday's in August." Maxzyne pokes her in the arm. "See? You are different! Just knowing you're four months older than me now, huh?"

Elise considers this observation carefully. "Well . . . maybe . . . yes."

Maxzyne opens her arms, taking in the vast selection of sweet delights. "Anyway, I think you should try one of everything, just to make up for lost time." She picks up the Easter basket she had filled with goodies earlier.

"Here, try one of these." She hands Elise a lollipop from her Easter basket. "It's not exactly a birthday present but . . ." She looks around again, thinking hard. "Hey! I have an idea! Stay right there," Maxzyne orders.

Elise stiffens, raising her eyebrows.

"Oops. There goes Miss Bossypants again, huh?"

"And I'm eleven now. You can't boss me around." Elise crams more cake into her mouth.

"Okay, would you like to sit down and I'll make you a special soda?" Maxzyne bows deeply from the waist.

"Much better." Elise wipes her mouth with the back of her hand. She nods.

Maxzyne grins, rising to kneel awkwardly on her high stool. "Great! My favorite's butterscotch. So if I remember how the guy makes it, bet you'll like it, too."

She clumsily climbs over the counter.

"Maxzyne! Be careful."

Pink cellophane bags tied with yellow satin ribbons scatter everywhere as Maxzyne knocks the display with her knee. One of the bags breaks open, sending jelly beans and yellow marshmallow chicks bouncing across the counter. A few fall to the floor.

"Uh, oh. Hey, might as well try those, too," she urges, dropping down on the other side of the counter. "Those peeps will be gone after Easter!"

Elise catches jellybeans with her mouth, giggling when she misses and they fall to the floor. Lining up the yellow chicks in a neat row, she pops them into her mouth, one by one. She pauses to bite the head off one, watching as Maxzyne takes down two tall soda glasses from the high shelf nearby. Hunting for the butterscotch flavor, the young soda clerk reads labels from the old-fashioned bottles standing on a silver revolving tray.

"Raspberry . . . coconut . . . chocolate . . . caramel . . . lemon—okay, here we go!"

Lifting out the bottle marked "Butterscotch," Maxzyne places it on the counter, holding a soda glass to the shiny silver spout. She pushes down on the lever and the spout squirts light brown syrup into the glass. "One . . . two . . . three . . . and . . . that's it," she counts. Returning the butterscotch bottle to its tray, she chooses another marked "Vanilla." Making

another squirt into the tall glass, she again counts, "One . . ." She smiles at Elise. "Three butterscotch, plus one vanilla. That's the recipe." She holds the tall glass high, admiring the amber, liquid drizzles. "See? This is easy. You know, I should probably work here when I grow up."

"I thought you were going to be an artist," Elise reminds her, licking a lollipop. The gold cupcake plate is empty, except for the candles and crumpled paper liner.

"Hey, maybe I'll do both!" Behind the counter, Maxzyne pushes a black lever on the soda fountain. With a great whoosh, fizzy water bursts from the silver spout below, bouncing to the bottom of the glass and then upward, right into her face. "Help! I can't turn it off!" She swats at the spray of water, which turns into a waterfall streaming over the counter.

Elise watches helplessly as a display of gummy bears and sour balls melts into a bubbling, colorful mess.

Both girls fumble frantically with the buttons behind the counter. They are relieved when the water finally shuts off. "I'm swimming in it!" Maxzyne groans, wiping her eyes.

With one arm, Elise sweeps the remaining chicks and jellybeans into Maxzyne's basket, saving them from the flood. "You're soaked! You look like . . ." She begins to laugh.

"My hair! No, not my hair!" Maxzyne squawks, rubbing her face with her denim jacket sleeve. Grabbing a paper napkin, she frantically blots her braids dry.

Elise falls over in a fit of giggles. She snorts, hiding her mouth behind the huge lollipop when Maxzyne scowls at her.

"Oh, very funny," Maxzyne huffs. Giving up, she pulls her braids high under her cap. "I want fizz, I get frizz—go figure." Securing her hat over her braids, she points to Elise. "No more laughing! I was making this for you, sister!"

"Still want a job here?" Elise asks, smirking. Then, realizing what Maxzyne has just said, she gasps. "That's—how did you know my wish, Maxzyne?"

Maxzyne is dumbfounded. "I did?"

"You just called me 'sister' didn't you?"

"Well, I . . . yeah, okay. Sure. I mean, why not? Sister's just slang for friend, and we're friendly, right?"

Elise nods energetically.

"So you're looking at your sister, Sister!" Maxzyne declares with a huge grin. "Hey, Sis! Shake on it?" She offers her hand.

Elise shakes her hand, beaming. "I'm so happy, Maxzyne! Before I met you, I never had a birthday, made a wish, or dreamed I'd have a sister. This is the most amazing day ever."

"And I never had a big sister before," Maxzyne answers solemnly. "And even if you are four months older, we have a lot in common, don't we? Fashion . . . music . . . and, of course, imagination!"

Elise nods. "And don't forget, cupcakes."

"And we both like adventure!" Maxzyne declares, returning to the soda fountain. "Now if I can just get this to work." She presses down very, very gently and pushes the rim of the soda glass under the spout. A gentle stream of bubbles trickles into the glass.

"I never had an adventure before, either," Elise says, popping a red jelly bean into her mouth. "What will happen next?"

"What will happen next? Well," Maxzyne says matter-of-factly, "we try not to let Mr. Tracy catch us. At least 'til we can get Gigi to see you're—well, she can't use your heads for her art . . ."

Elise shudders, nearly choking as she coughs the jelly bean into her hand.

Maxzyne quickly changes the subject. "Anyway,

one scoop of vanilla ice cream, and you'll know it's the best soda you ever had," she promises. "It'll be sodalicious!"

"So delicious?"

"No. Sodalicious! Get it?"

"Is that truly a word, Maxzyne?"

"Of course not. I just made it up. My language arts teacher, Ms. Clark, says made-up words are usually funny words like 'sodalicious.' They're not in the dictionary, but they could be. They're called 'sniglets.'"

"You mean we could even have our own language? Make up our own words?" Elise is thrilled.

"Sure. Why should grown-ups get to make up all the words?" Maxzyne reaches for the silver ice cream scoop. Like this—it could be a 'scroop.' Sort of shorthand for ice cream scoop."

"Yes! Or . . . Elise looks around the room. She points at the melted candy mess on the floor. "I know! Marshuddle! A puddle of marshmallow, right?"

"Yeah, that works. Okay. Here's one." Maxzyne cracks open the freezer chest, letting the icy mist swirl in the warm air. "Frair." Elise looks puzzled. "Frair! You know, frozen air!"

"Oh! Yes, that's perfect! This is fun. Can I make up another one?"

"Sure, knock yourself out."

"Hit myself?"

"Uh, that's not a sniglet, that's just slang. Like 'go

for it,' Elise. You know the difference, right?"

"I think so." She twirls her ponytail, thinking. "But if you had a sniglet AND a slang word, it could be a slinglet!" she suggests, laughing.

"Oh, Elise! You sniggled!" Maxzyne falls over with a bad case of giggles. The two girls can hardly look at each other.

"Sniggle!" Elise repeats, bending double with laughter until she snorts and gasps for breath.

Maxzyne grins, holding her sides. "Don't snort! I can't stop laughing!" She wipes her eyes, gasping. "I can't believe it! I laughed so hard I cried!"

Once the girls catch their breath, Maxzyne picks up the ice cream scoop. "Now back to that ice cream soda." She disappears behind the counter, her head in the freezer as the cold air rises around her. Elise kneels on the high, striped stool, leaning over the counter to watch Maxzyne scrape ice cream from the circular carton with her scoop. "Whew! It's sure a lot harder than it looks." Slamming the freezer chest closed, she uses her finger to pry the ice cream blob from the metal scoop. It drops with a small splash into the glass. Like magic, the amber soda water fizzes and bubbles, rising around the ice cream.

Elise is fascinated. "It's noisy and growing bigger! Are you sure it's safe to drink?"

Maxzyne laughs, holding up a thin, silver container. "Not without whipped cream, you don't!"

Pointing the nozzle at the floating mound of ice cream, she creates a smiley face of whipped cream swirls.

"It looks like new snow," Elise marvels, swiping a frothy tendril with one finger and licking. "Mmmmm . . . It tastes like sweet . . . air?"

"Hey, it's not done 'til the cherry's on top!" Maxzyne drops a fat, red cherry half in the center of the smiley face. Then she steps back to admire her work.

"You are definitely an artist," Elise declares, picking up the towering drink. Not sure what to do, she sinks her mouth into the whipped cream topping and slurps. As she does, some of the amber liquid sloshes out of the glass and into her lap.

"Oh!" Elise gasps. "It's cold!"

"Elise! You can't drink it like that!"

"Huh?" Elise raises her head, perplexed. Her pale chin drips with whipped cream, and the cherry sticks to her nose.

"Oh, my gosh! You should see your face! Now that's what I call a 'chwipnose.'"

"What's that? Oh, don't make me start laughing again!"

"Cherry and whipped cream nose," answers Maxzyne. Another giggle bursts forth, making Elise snort again, before the two finally calm down. "Here. Guess I forgot these." Maxzyne holds out a striped straw and long silver spoon. "Now put one end in the glass and the other in your mouth and suck!"

"Oooh, the bubbles tickle my tongue!" gasps Elise. She sets the glass down and wipes her face with a napkin. "But I like it." She smiles, smacking her lips. "Are you having one?"

"Uh . . . yeah. I'm going to try something different this time."

Between slurps from the straw, Elise daintily spoons ice cream into her mouth. Maxzyne sprays another soda glass with drizzles of yellow, blue, red, and orange.

"That's pretty."

"Lemon, blueberry, peppermint, orange," Maxzyne announces with each squirt. She holds the tall glass up to the light and twirls. "Cool, huh?"

Elise nods, her mouth full, lips puckered around the straw. Maxzyne carefully pushes the glass against the soda fountain spout. The girls watch the bubbly water fill the glass, colors swirling. After a minute, the soda bubbles turn the liquid a muddy, unappealing brown.

"Yuck!" Maxzyne frowns, looking at the glass. "I should have remembered from art class—too many colors makes brown."

Elise wrinkles her nose. "Will it taste better than it looks?"

"Maybe with chocolate ice cream, some malt balls, and cocoa sprinkles, since it's already brown,"

Maxzyne decides, picking up the metal scoop.

Elise nods, busily slurping the last of her butterscotch soda from the tall glass.

Maxzyne ducks into the freezer chest again. She emerges grinning and holding a fat scoop of chocolate ice cream. She plops it into her glass. Together the girls watch the soda fizz and rise into a foamy brown cloud. At the last minute, they add cocoa sprinkles and malt balls.

"Don't forget the whipped cream," Elise reminds her. "And a cherry."

"Who's Miss Bossypants Big Sister now?" Maxzyne teases, squirting the other girl with a burst of whipped cream from the silver container.

Elise chuckles, licking the frothy swirl from the shoulder of her badly stained dress.

Adding several cherry bits to the towering creation, Maxzyne arranges them in a circle around the cream-covered rim. "Now that's a masterpiece!" she declares, holding the glass high. Thick brown liquid sloshes over the edge, onto the counter.

"You mean a 'Maxerpiece'!" Elise claps her hands.

Maxzyne lowers the glass, inserts the straw, closes her eyes, and takes a long sip.

"Do you like it?" Elise asks, waiting.

"Mmm. I'm not sure. Kind of, I guess. But it doesn't taste like anything I ever had before." She takes another sip, considering. "Still, it's an original, right?

My own flavor. I'll call it the 'Maxzyne!'" Happily slurping, she spoons chunks of chocolate ice cream, malt balls, and cream-covered cherry chunks into her mouth. Then she fishes into the drink with her fingers. "Share?" she asks, plucking out a slippery malt ball.

Elise shakes her head, cringing a little.

Shrugging, Maxzyne pops the chocolate into her own mouth, crunching loudly. "More for me, I guess."

"Buuuurrrp!" Embarrassed, Elise covers her mouth. "Something's wrong, Maxzyne!" she cries. "My tummy feels funny." She bends over, clutching her stomach. "I don't feel good!"

"That's just the bubbles, Elise. Just burp a few more times. Girls aren't supposed to, but you'll feel better. I won't tell anyone."

"Are you sure? How do I do it again? It just came out."

"Like this." Taking in a big gulp of air, Maxzyne opens her mouth wide, waiting.

"Buuuuuuuuurrrrrrpp!"

Elise looks impressed. "That was a good one!"

Maxzyne beams with pride. "Yeah, but Mother would've sent me to my room, for sure. It's considered bad manners."

"Maman would not approve then, either. But I do feel terrible!"

"The boys at school burp at lunch sometimes, just to gross out the girls."

Elise takes a deep breath. She waits, her mouth open wide. "Buuuurrrp!" After a few seconds, she says with relief, "Oh, you're right. I do feel better!"

"Contest!" Maxzyne announces. "Who can burp the loudest?" She opens her mouth wide, letting loose. "Buuuurp!"

Elise challenges her, gulping more air into her lungs. "Buuuuurp! I win!"

"Okay, how 'bout the longest?" Maxzyne urges. "Winner gets another chocolate bunny!"

"Buuuuuuuuuuurrrrrrrrrrrrrrrrrrrp!" The girls exhale loudly at the same time, squeezing their tummies for the last bit of air.

"Tie!" Maxzyne decrees, giving Elise a fist bump.

"I love being a real girl!" Elise says, beaming. "And having a sister! It's so much fun!"

"Hey, don't forget your prize." Maxzyne offers her a chocolate bunny, just as a ball of pale fur bursts into the room.

"Peppin!" shrieks Elise. "What are you doing here?"

The poodle leaps, licking her face and whimpering. Elise listens and then covers her mouth in dismay.

"*Que c'est-il passé?*" (What happened?) Peppin responds with high-pitched yelps. Elise jumps down from the stool. "We have to go! Right now! Maman and Papa think we've been caught, and Ray knows I'm missing from the window. We've got to get back right now and—"

"What is going on down here?" a familiar nasal voice demands from the shadows. "Just who gave you permission to be here after hours?"

Gasping, the girls turn to see Mr. Tracy glaring over the banister of the stairwell landing. The blood drains from his face when he sees the dripping soda mess, bedraggled ribbons, and cellophane candy wrappers strewn about the floor and counter. His eyes bulge, taking in the empty cupcake plate, dirty soda glasses, half-melted candles, and oozing candy mess.

"How dare you! You've ruined our Easter display! Tomorrow is the biggest candy sale day of the season!" he yells, running down the stairs. Reaching the last step, he watches Peppin snuffling for chocolate tidbits in an overturned Easter basket. "You little hooligans! Why, I'm going to—"

Reaching frantically into his pocket, he pulls out a cell phone. His bow tie wobbles with indignation. "We'll take care of this!" Frozen, the girls watch him dial a number. "Get me security now!" he yells into the phone.

Black eyebrows meet like two fuzzy caterpillars on his high forehead, jerking up and down as he waits on the phone. He pulls a blue, silk handkerchief from his pocket and wipes his sweaty face. "Look at this mess!" the manager yells, waving the crumpled silk at the melting sweets dripping down the counter.

As he strides toward the girls, candies crunch and ooze beneath his shiny shoes. He stops, frowning in disgust, trying to step around the mess, and glaring at the muddy footprints he leaves on the tile floor. His pale face turns pink, and then red, the color deepening until it nearly matches his purple shirt.

His thin moustache vibrating with anger, he snarls into the phone. "Jameson, get down here! I've caught them! Our two vandals—right here in front of me! So tell me, what do I pay you for? Yeah! Lower level! I want their parents notified and billed for damages. Somebody's going to pay! Do you hear me?" He pauses, listening. "What's that? Police? No, they're just kids. I think we can handle it," he retorts, squinting at the two girls. "Why aren't you here already? Make it happen—NOW!"

Catching the manager off guard, Peppin leaps forward, growling menacingly. He bares his teeth, nipping at a pants leg.

Mr. Tracy kicks at him in rage. "Get out of my way, mutt!" He tries to walk backward, but slips in the puddle again. "Call your dog off! You hear me?" he croaks, reaching to free his pant leg. "That's designer, you beast!"

Clutching the phone, he waves his handkerchief at Peppin like a mad bullfighter. Man and dog do a crazy dance, darting at each other, until Mr. Tracy slips in the goo, falling to one knee. The silk handkerchief flutters to the floor, slowly turning a dark shade of brown as it soaks up candy ooze. Sensing victory, Peppin backs away toward the counter, pausing just long enough to gulp down a chocolate bunny paw he finds on the floor.

"Look what you've done!" the outraged manager screams. "You'll pay for this!" Panting and gasping, he wipes buttercream mint from one knee.

Elise is the first to recover her wits. Maxzyne watches, still frozen in shock, as the other girl springs into action and begins climbing over the counter. Peppin quickly follows. He leaps onto a stool, landing behind the counter with a muffled thud.

"Come on, Maxzyne! Quick! In that door," Elise hisses, pointing. "Over there—past the lollipops!"

Finally jolted into action, Maxzyne slips and slides past the soda fountain, scrambling after Peppin and Elise. They crawl toward the lollipop stand, half slithering on their knees through the slush on the messy floor. Peppin sometimes pauses for a quick lick at a sticky tidbit. Pushing the lollipop display aside, Elise scrambles toward a small, cleverly hidden wood door, wrenching it open.

"In here!" she calls in a loud whisper as she reaches for Peppin, who desperately scrabbles and jumps at the wall, trying to get inside.

"*C'est bien* (It's okay)," Elise reassures the dog. She gives him a quick boost, heaving him inside, before ducking her own head and crawling inside.

Hearing the manager huff and puff as he strains to reach them from the other side of the counter, Maxzyne grabs the door handle and lunges into the small, cramped space. She crouches next to Elise and Peppin, her eyes adjusting to the dark. "What is this? We'll be trapped in here, Elise!"

"No, no! It moves! Up and down! See? It's kind of like a little elevator." Elise yanks hard on a rope above her head, and the floor of their escape hatch suddenly tilts sideways.

"Watch it!" Maxzyne clutches at the side wall. "Maybe it's not safe!"

"Don't worry! Pull that other rope when I pull mine." Maxzyne has never seen Elise so sure of herself. Obeying, she grabs the rope next to her and pulls. The floor under their feet lurches crazily again, and the two girls and the dog slide into a heap. "No, no! Wait 'til I tell you," Elise commands.

"Elise! Are you sure this thing is okay?"

"Believe me." Elise speaks in a rushed whisper. "I remember it from when I was in the display. The boys who worked down here used to fool around with it, and when the display was finished, they put Peppin and me inside it and took us up to the main floor. I think they called it the dumbwaiter."

"If you say so!" Maxzyne eyes the ropes passing over pulleys above them, leading into the darkness.

Can she trust this strange and spooky contraption? *Breathe*. She nods, breathing out slowly. "Okay then, let me count and when I get to three, we pull at the same time. Ready?"

"Ready."

"One, two, THREE!"

The compartment begins to rise, carrying them upward, less tipsy this time, but slow. As they go up, they hear crashing and thumping from outside the dumbwaiter shaft below. *It must be Mr. Tracy falling behind the counter,* Maxzyne thinks, trying not to giggle.

There is more thrashing and an angry, muffled shout as the girls rise higher in the dark. "My new phone! My pants! My—I'll get you for this! You can't get away! There's nowhere to hide! SECURITY!" There is another thump as the manager screams. "Help! SEEEEECCCCCCURRRRRRITY!"

11

Teamwork

MAXZYNE'S HEART POUNDS. Where are they going? This whole contraption, this so-called dumbwaiter, seems rickety and dangerous. But if she can focus on pulling as steadily as possible, maybe she can stay calm. *Breathe.*

"One, two, THREE." Gradually falling into a regular rhythm, the girls take turns counting to three, and slowly, in bursts, the old-fashioned lift creeps higher. Beside them, poor Peppin shakes violently, feet always shifting to stay balanced. Each time the girls pull on the ropes, he gives a sorrowful whine.

"*Calme-tu!* (Be calm!)" Elise says gently. With a final howl, the dog sits down, panting in the dark.

"One, two, THREE! One, two, THREE!" Progress is slow. Maxzyne's shoulders and hands ache until she can't pull anymore. "Wait a minute," she gasps. Panting, each girl clings to her rope, resting in the pitch dark. Hanging somewhere between two floors, Maxzyne tries not to think of bats and spiders.

Elise is first to resume the count. "Ready? One, two, THREE! One, two, THREE!" With each determined pull of the rope, her voice remains steady. "No time to waste."

Hands burning from working the coarse rope, Maxzyne squints, peering through the shadows overhead. What's that crack of light? Her heart skips a beat when she sees a square outline about 30 feet above. Could it be a way out? "I think I see a light, Elise! Maybe it's a door. Just four more pulls!" *I don't care where it goes,* she thinks. *Just get me out of here.*

Peppin scrambles to his feet. His wagging tail brushes against Maxzyne's leg.

"Good! Let's hope the door's not locked from the other side on the main level," Elise says, sounding relieved. "My hands hurt."

"I know. Mine, too. We're going to have major blisters."

Chanting together, the two girls pull with newfound strength. "One, two, THREE. One, two, THREE!" They lower their voices as the light grows nearer.

"I'm so glad you're with me, Elise. I'd hate to be hanging in the dark all by myself."

"Me, too. It's always better to stick together."

"Yeah, teamwork. Right, Peppin?"

Peppin gives a soft yelp, his fluffy tail wagging against Maxzyne's leg again.

"Oh, no! He wants more chocolate," Elise laughs.

How can anyone think of eating at a time like this? Maxzyne wonders. She peers overhead, trying to judge the distance between them and the light. "I think we're getting close," she whispers, winded after a hard pull. "We can make it."

"Just three more pulls," Elise pants. Exhausted, she hangs on to her rope, allowing them both to rest a moment.

Peppin sniffs, growing impatient. With an excited whimper, he rises on his hind legs, wanting out.

"*Pas encore* (Not yet), Peppin," Elise cautions. "Stay! You'll get hurt." With an anguished groan, he sits obediently.

"One, two, THREE. One, two, THREE. One, two, THREE!" they whisper hoarsely. At last, they stop. The light shining through the half-cracked trapdoor makes them blink. Sniffing and panting, Peppin jumps forward, pushing with his paws. The door swings open, making a terrible, high-pitched squeak.

"Wait, Peppin!" Maxzyne warns. "What happens if we let go of the rope, Elise? We won't go crashing back down, will we?"

Elise nods, looking at the ropes and pulleys above them. "You're right. We better let go at the same time and everybody jump out together. Okay?" She rests one knee against the dog. "Stay, Peppin."

Gripping her rope, Maxzyne moves toward the door and pokes her head out. The area is quiet and peaceful. Racks of handbags and gaily patterned silk scarves stand in the shadowy gloom. She ducks back inside the dumbwaiter.

"The coast is clear. Just purses and scarves."

"Okay, here we go!" Elise orders. "Now!" The three leap from the dumbwaiter, bursting through the trapdoor, and landing in a heap on the floor. Maxzyne quickly jumps up to close the door to their escape hatch. "Makes it harder for them to track us." She rubs her sore hands on her skirt, wincing. Then she turns them over to examine her blisters.

"Good idea. We have escaped to the accessories department!" Elise says. "Oh! Let's not forget Maman's shawl."

"No time to shop 'til you drop, Elise. We're on a mission, remember? Okay, single file, army style—follow me!"

Elise pulls on Maxzyne's arm, stopping her at the

open door. "*I'm* the big sister, remember? That means I'm—"

"Oh, all right," Maxzyne sighs. "It's your birthday. You go first, then." But Peppin bursts ahead.

"Peppin! *Attente!* (Wait!)" Elise hisses.

Ignoring her, Peppin disappears under a rack of sparkling evening bags. There is a tinkling sound as the purses swing wildly on their gold chains.

"He'll get caught, Maxzyne!"

"It's okay, Elise. He's quick and knows where to go. He found us, didn't he?"

"You're right," Elise agrees. "Ray's already looking for me, so if Peppin's back in the window where he belongs, he might think Gigi took me out." She blows on her red palms. "At least only one of us will be missing." She drops to the floor. "We better crawl so we don't get noticed."

As Maxzyne drops to her knees, her necklace escapes her jacket collar. "Yikes! Don't need this giving us away, either." She drops the little bell into her mouth, silencing it. Head bowed, she follows Elise, but her braids fall forward and her hat tumbles to the floor.

"Maxzyne! Can't you get yourself together? We don't have much time!" Elise complains. Turning, she picks up the hat and hands it to Maxzyne, who quickly tucks her braids back under the brim.

"Shhh! Did you hear that?"

They listen for a minute. Nothing.

"Quick, over here. Just in case." Maxzyne crawls under the nearest display of long, silk scarves and disappears into a shimmering cloud. Elise follows close behind as the fringed shawls fall back into place behind them. They sit quietly, listening.

"Elise, we could be princesses in a silk tent, like in *Aladdin*," Maxzyne whispers, pulling a navy scarf from the rack. She drapes it over her head like a veil until only her eyes show. "Any minute there will be a flying carpet with a prince coming to rescue us!"

"But *you're* supposed to rescue us, remember?" Elise reminds her. She reaches over and pulls the tiny gold chain with the bell. Its chimes ring softly. "Maxzyne! Calling Maxzyne!"

"Oh, yeah. *Me* to the rescue!" With a self-conscious laugh, Maxzyne pulls the scarf from her head and face. "Okay, getting to the window from here . . . it's that way, right?" She points across the huge expanse of sales floor, nudging Elise.

"Wait! Someone's coming," Elise whispers.

They both freeze. Afraid to breathe out, they listen as footsteps cross the marble floor, reach the plush carpeting near their hiding place, and grow silent.

"We're going to find 'em, Mr. Tracy."

Oh, no! Jameson! With thumping hearts, the two girls listen as the trapdoor opens and shuts.

"I swear, I can smell 'em, boss."

"You'd better find them, Jameson. Letting two kids make fools of us!"

Horrified, the girls cower in their silken hideaway. The carpet rustles as Mr. Tracy comes closer, stopping to lean against their display. Maxzyne shivers when his ruined shoes stop just inches from the swaying fringe. She holds both hands against her chest. Can he hear the tremendous thud, thud, thud of her heart?

"Hey! See that? It's their dog! Get him, Jameson! Quick! Do something right for once!"

There is the sound of racing footsteps, jangling purses, and the skittering of Peppin's toenails on smooth marble.

"Peppin must have doubled back to throw them off our trail, Elise! I think he's drawing them to the fountain, where he can hide under the plants like we did earlier." Elise bites her knuckle fearfully.

"He's mine!" Jameson shouts. There is a sharp bark and the sound of splashing. "Not to worry, boss! Got him trapped! He's in the fountain, and I'm about to grab him!"

"You'd better if you want to keep your job! Those hoodlums and that dog ate my Easter display! Don't let that frou-frou little . . ." Suddenly, he sneezes. "Tell me I'm not getting a cold, now. All this stress! It's killing me! Ahhhh—choo! Those kids must be around here somewhere!" He stomps past their hiding place until his footsteps gradually fade.

Maxzyne and Elise hold hands. Silently, Maxzyne wills Peppin to escape. Seconds later, there is another bark and more splashing noises.

"I've got you!" Jameson crows, but then disappointment tinges his voice. "Oh, no! Hey! Back off, you, you—"

The girls grin, hearing a snarl, several yips, and skittering toenails on marble before they fade into the distance.

"Go, Peppin!" Maxzyne mouths silently.

Elise clutches Maxzyne's arm. Together, they lean forward, peering at Mr. Tracy from behind their filmy veil. With a snort, he slaps his palm against the dumbwaiter door. The girls shrink back into their hideaway when he begins searching the displays for them, angrily flinging scarves and purses.

Jameson returns, panting.

"Don't tell me you didn't get him!"

"Er, well, I had my hand on him," Jameson wheedles, "but the little monster tried to nip me!"

"Ahhhhhh–choooooo!" Mr. Tracy sneezes again. "Where's my handkerchief! Well, never mind the dog! Find those girls! I want them punished!"

The girls are horrified when a stubby hand reaches to pull a scarf from the display. Terrified, they squeeze their eyes closed, fearing the worst. Seconds later, there is a loud, honking noise as the scarf is used as a handkerchief. Maxzyne's eyes fly open, just in time to see the manager wipe his mustache and then crumple the large, silk square into his pocket.

"Uh, that's inventory, sir," Jameson reminds him. "Still got a tag on it."

"I don't need your inventory speech, Jameson! I want those girls caught!" the manager howls. The girls watch as the manager throws the soiled scarf on the counter and walks away. "Now!"

"I'm on it, boss." The sound of Jameson's running footsteps fades.

"Wait! Give me your phone, Jameson!" Mr. Tracy chases after the security detective. "Those hooligans ruined mine!" His voice fades. There is a sudden crash, a splash, and a loud groan of pain.

Maxzyne and Elise look at each other, mouths wide open in disbelief. *Did he just slip and fall into the fountain?*

"JAMESON! Get back here! Nowwww! I slipped! Did you hear me? And get the cleaners to mop this up before we get sued. I swear when I get my hands on those girls I'll— Ahhhhhh–chooooo!"

At last, the sound of squeaking shoes slowly fades away.

"Good old Peppin!" Maxzyne whispers. "He got the marble floor wet, and Mr. T. didn't stand a chance." She puts a hand over her mouth to keep from laughing out loud.

Elise nods, exchanging a weak fist bump with Maxzyne.

"It didn't sound like he broke any bones, did it? I mean, we don't want anybody getting hurt," Maxzyne worries. "Even if it's just an accident."

"But what about Peppin? Maxzyne, you don't think they'll catch him, do you?"

"Nah. He's got Jameson sidetracked. So while he's looking for Peppin, let's get back to the window. I bet Peppin's there already. Come on!"

Crawling from their hiding place, they see the damage that they have caused to yet another display. Although Mr. Tracy actually knocked everything over, Maxzyne knows they will be blamed. Worse, they think she and Elise are stealing! Her cheeks burn. "We're in big trouble, and I still haven't convinced Gigi to save your heads, Elise!" Her shoulders droop. "I just need to focus instead of . . ." Her voice trails off.

Elise nods silently, before bending to pluck a fallen silk shawl with pansies from the floor. She wraps it several times around her neck, knotting it firmly under her chin. Head high, she motions to Maxzyne, who quickly follows.

12

Sisters

"WATCH OUT, ELISE! There's water everywhere, so it's going to be slippery," Maxzyne warns. Elise stops, allowing Maxzyne to take the lead. Maxzyne steps carefully in her red suede boots, reaching for Elise's arm. But it's too late. The soles of her shoes already wet, Elise wobbles, nearly slipping, her smooth-soled Mary Janes skidding on the marble floor. Lunging forward, Maxzyne pulls her upright.

"Whew! Thanks, Maxzyne." Elise glances around the Great Hall, worried. "We have to get away from here. It's too exposed."

"Okay. But hold my hand, 'cause your shoes are wet. I promised to get you back to the window. Your parents will kill me if anything's broken." She pauses, looking at Elise.

"I know. It's just a figure of speech."

Elise gratefully clasps Maxzyne's sturdy brown hand. Afraid of being seen in the open, the girls skitter in the direction of the weeping Japanese plum tree and its treasure of costume jewelry. The after-hours lighting gives the delicate tree a frightening air. Branches snake down around the eerily glowing, white trellis, casting long shadows underneath. The crystal gems nestle on velvet pillows in their boxes, unable to sparkle in the faint light.

"Oh, dear. I hope nothing has happened. Maman and Papa must be so worried!" Elise whispers.

"I'm just glad we made it!" Maxzyne squeezes Elise's hand. "We had a few close calls, huh?"

Elise nods, her blonde hair falling loose across her face. Taking the lead, she makes a beeline for the heavy, white curtain on the far wall but suddenly stops.

Maxzyne brakes beside her, impatient at the delay. "What's up? We're almost there, Elise!"

Elise looks down, smoothing her soiled, wrinkled dress.

"What gives, Elise?" Maxzyne throws her hands up.

Elise nervously pulls her hair back, letting it settle in a soft cloud around her shoulders. Her face solemn, she finally meets Maxzyne's gaze.

"C'mon, already! We're here! What are you waiting for?"

"I know. I just—I just . . . well, thank you."

"Huh? For what? I almost got us caught five times, remember?"

Elise smiles. "I know. But when I wasn't scared half to death, really; it was the most fun I've ever had. I mean, ever will have, now that I'm back at our window, I suppose." She looks sadly around.

"Okay, I admit—me, too," Maxzyne replies. "How cool that I got to have an adventure with you—"

"—and I had a birthday!" Elise rises gracefully on her toes, leaning over to take Maxzyne's hand. "And made my first sister-friend ever."

"Firsis, you mean."

Elise nods. "Forever firsis."

Grinning, Maxzyne squeezes Elise's hand and then starts a fist bump.

"I'll never forget you, ever, Maxzyne," Elise promises softly.

"We're family now, aren't we?"

Elise grins shyly. "Promise?"

"Forever. Even if you are older than me now, you're my best friend!" She gives her a gentle, awkward hug. Swallowing hard, she steps back. "Of course, I still have to save you from you-know-who." She adjusts the black cap on her forehead, thinking. "You know, back there? In the ladies' room? Gigi didn't sound as scary as she looks. At least, not as scary as I thought she'd be, what with cutting heads off stuff and all . . ."

Her voice trails off when she sees the sick look on

Elise's face. "Sorry! Forget I said anything! Back to the parents, huh?"

Nodding in relief, Elise walks toward the white curtain.

From the corner of her eye, Maxzyne notices a pile of old alarm clocks heaped on the floor by the curtain. "Hey!" she points. "What are those doing here?"

"Oh, no! Are we too late?" Elise gasps. Yanking the curtain aside, she rushes into the window. "Maman! Papa! Are you here?"

13

Alone Again

"**MAMAN! PAPA!** Please, are you—?" Elise does not wait for Maxzyne. She disappears through the curtain.

"Oh, Elise! It is you! *C'est vrai!* (It is true!) We were so worried. Thank goodness!"

There is a joyful bark from Peppin. Three voices scold, "*Chut!* (Quiet!)"

Maxzyne carefully enters the window. The white curtain falls in place behind her. "Peppin, you're okay!" She grins in relief. "See, Elise, I told you he—" Maxzyne stops, distracted by the changes made to the window while she and Elise were gone. She notes that the redecoration has begun and that the furniture has been pushed to one side. People walking past will most likely think the mannequins are either store models or workers redoing the display. Certainly not mannequins who have come

146

to life by some kind of crazy magic!

"*Oui*, Peppin told us all about your little adventure. So there is no use denying it, *mes enfants* (children)," Aloin warns. He looks at Veronique. "Cakes and candies, the discovery by Mr. Tracy, the escape in the dumbwaiter, and—let's not forget—the chase."

"Oh, *non*—just look at your clothes!" Veronique points at the two girls.

Ashamed, they look down at the floor.

"And poor Peppin nearly caught his death of a cold, in that—that spill he took in the fountain. Didn't he, Aloin?"

Aloin nods grimly. "Elise, I never should have let you go. Didn't you listen when I warned you to be careful? I thought you were to be trust—"

"B-b-but it's not fair to blame her, Mr. French. Really," Maxzyne stammers. "Stuff happens sometimes. It's not her fault."

"Of course we blame her," Veronique says. "She is a mannequin and knows what is allowed and what is not! She was raised a proper French *jeune fille* (young girl) and knows that she is to always look her best in whatever position or window she is placed. That is her purpose, and her place is here with us. *N'est-ce pas* (Isn't it), Elise?" Veronique gives her daughter a withering stare.

Elise hangs her head.

In an instant, Maxzyne understands Elise's

constricted life. *How frustrating to always watch from a window but never have adventures of your own,* she thinks. *And I complain about the kid maximum security protection program!*

Now poor Elise is getting blamed for Maxzyne's imagination gone wild: the hats, the music, the birthday party. "You can't be mad at her. She saved the day! She and Peppin both! You should've seen her in the dumbwaiter! If she hadn't been there, we never would've—"

"Never would have been caught in the first place, if you had listened to me." Aloin sighs, turning to scold his daughter. "Remember? I told you that being real brings the possibility for real trouble. Too much time has been wasted with your silly escapades. Now we are truly in danger. I don't know what will happen." He shakes his head.

"I'm sorry, Papa," Elise whispers. She turns to her mother. "Maman, can you forgive me?" Elise unwraps the pretty shawl from around her neck. She drapes it gently around her mother's shoulders.

Unable to stay silent, Maxzyne steps forward, waving her arms. "Hey! It wasn't her fault, people! You can't blame her. It was me!"

"YOU!" Veronique hisses. She is shaking with fury. "We trusted you to keep her safe! You promised to help us! Instead YOU are nothing but trouble!" Veronique glares at Maxzyne. She points toward the curtain, willing her to leave.

Elise steps between Veronique and Maxzyne. "No! Please, Maman! Maxzyne is my sister and my friend! She even gave me a birthday party. Because of her, I'm eleven. She showed me how to burp and make up words and play the piano and—"

"ENOUGH!" Aloin shouts, his pale face turning red. He unbuttons his tight collar and takes a deep breath before speaking. "Let us be calm, ladies." From the floor, Peppin whines. "And gentleman, Peppin," Aloin adds. "Mademoiselle Maxzyne, you have brought Elise back. For that we are grateful. However, we are still in danger. I am not sure how you can help, given it is your silly nature to become distracted and to play games. But you are all we have. Unless you can change Gigi's mind about using us for her exhibit, I'm afraid you will lose your sister and friend. Forever."

Veronique gasps. She twists the shawl in her hands. "*Oui*, it is true. And Ray has discovered Elise missing. So already it is too late!"

Aloin interrupts. "But I heard him say that he thinks Gigi has taken our Elise. So perhaps there is still a chance."

Maxzyne eagerly pounces on this information. "That means Elise should come with me!" Stunned, they all stare at her as if she's crazy.

"What?" Aloin asks.

"If she's already missing, she should stay missing.

Right? That way, Mr. Tracy, Jameson, or whoever won't know why she's missing from the window, and they'll waste time trying to figure it out. In the meantime, I find Gigi and tell her the truth. And if Elise is with me, seeing is believing."

"Believing what?" Aloin asks. He is doubtful of any wild plans that include Elise again.

"That you're all real!" Maxzyne exclaims. "It's better if Gigi sees the truth for herself," she insists. "And even if she comes to the window before *we* find *her*, sir, you should just . . . well, be yourselves. Your real selves, I mean."

Veronique shakes her head. She shivers and pulls the shawl tight around her shoulders.

Maxzyne continues. "That's it! Talk, move around, show her . . . your goose bumps, your French, your, you know, everything."

Before anyone can answer, they hear a scratching noise over by the window. They turn to see Peppin whine and claw at the heavy plate glass.

"What is it, boy?" They all rush to the window. To their surprise, they see Esmeralda next to the glass. She is sitting on her battered suitcase. Her red cape falls from her shoulders as she shakes and moans.

"It's Esmeralda!" Elise exclaims. "Something's wrong! Peppin? Did you see? What happened to her?"

Between Peppin's barks and whines, Elise translates. "She was eating . . . a candy bar someone gave her and—" Upset, she makes a perfect "O" with her mouth. "No! She's not supposed to have sugar because it's bad for her!" Strangely, Elise's mouth suddenly stops moving. There is a strangling noise, as if she can't get the words out, and then silence. Her whole body seems to freeze.

"Elise? What's wrong? What's bad about sugar? Tell me!" Maxzyne grabs Elise by the shoulders. She looks to Aloin and Veronique for help, but they, too, are frozen in place. Even Peppin sits silent and still, one paw pressed against the window. Maxzyne shakes Elise by the arm, but her pink, rosebud mouth remains frozen in a half circle. The sparkle has dimmed in her wide blue eyes.

"Elise! What is it? Mr. French! What's wrong with you guys?" She pulls desperately on Aloin's jacket. "Talk to me!" she begs, her eyes filling with tears. "Somebody, say something—anything. Even you," she pleads, turning to Veronique. "Go on, say something French. Scold me for messing up. Please?" Maxzyne waits, but there is no response. She is alone.

Maxzyne picks up the delicate shawl that has slipped through Veronique's frozen fingers and landed on the floor. She carefully places it around the mannequin's shoulders. She sniffles, trying to read the woman's proud, frozen face. "I know you're in there. Just tell me what to do and I'll do it!" she begs. "Right away this time. I promise!"

Outside, there is a loud thump on the window. Esmeralda is shaking where she lies half-slumped against the window. She seems to be having a kind of seizure. The red hood falls away from her face. It exposes a blue, wool stocking cap that partially covers long, fuzzy braids tied at the ends with bits of string and twist ties. Esmeralda looks thin and weak without her woolen layer.

"Esmeralda!" Maxzyne pounds on the glass.

Maxzyne sees someone cross Randolph Street. "Help! You have to help her!" she cries. She bangs harder on the window. However, the stranger walks on toward the river and disappears from view.

"Esmeralda . . ." Maxzyne breathes in ragged gulps, trying to figure things out. "What's happened to you? And why aren't Elise and the others real anymore? Did your seizure turn them back into mannequins again? What do I do now? How can I help?"

Struggling for answers, she runs back to Aloin. His loose collar gives him a sloppy look that he would not want anyone to see. Gently, Maxzyne reaches to button it. But when her fingers touch his smooth, cold skin, she backs away in horror. She nearly topples him. Even as he wobbles, he still looks as though he's disappointed in her. "Hey!" she shouts. "I'm just ten! How do you expect me to know what to do?"

There is no answer except his frozen stare.

Maxzyne runs to Elise. "Elise! How do I help Esmeralda and get you back again? Somebody? Tell me!"

14

Call for Help

"**I**'VE GOT TO WAKE Esmeralda," Maxzyne decides. "Somehow. There must be a way." Esmeralda seems to be the key to everything about the mannequins. So she's got to save the homeless woman. Maxzyne glances around the display area, searching for something that might help.

A quick scan uncovers the oversized, glittering Easter egg lying beside Veronique's armchair. But that's no use. It's just papier-mâché. Kicking it, Maxzyne watches it roll over to the window. Is there anything useful in the Easter basket? She dumps the contents. But there's nothing of any use except the champagne bottle. Should she smash the window with it? *No. Terrible idea.* Alarms would go off. The police would come. She'd definitely go to jail. Okay. She'll break the window only if she can't think of anything else. But there must be another way. *Breathe! Think!* Crossing her arms, she paces back and forth, pausing to check on Esmeralda. What does it mean if she's no longer shaking but still not awake?

"Oh, please wake up, Esmeralda!" Maxzyne slaps the plate glass window with her palms.

"Dad always says, when you've got a problem, break it down to find the solution," she declares. She thinks of her father at his desk, watching computer screens, making deals around the clock. *That's it! The clocks!*

Maxzyne runs to the back of the display area. She pulls aside the heavy, white curtain. The strange assortment of old brass clocks remains stacked nearby. Nobody is in sight. She scurries over and selects three of the biggest from the pile. "Bigger is louder," she reasons. Darting back through the curtain, she runs to the window, kneels, and begins winding the largest clock. She is relieved when it begins to tick.

"Okay. Get ready to tick-tock! Eight o'clock!"

Maxzyne twists the clock hands to the eight o'clock position. Then she sets the mechanical alarm. A minute later she has set the other two clocks. She lines them up against the window, so close they could touch Esmeralda through the glass. Then she waits impatiently. The clocks tick loudly for several seconds. Suddenly, the brass alarm bells sound, pulsing against the glass with loud, metallic shrieks.

"C'mon, Esmeralda. Wake up!" Maxzyne pleads. She waits, watching for any sign of movement. "Please! We need you to wake up!" She rests her forehead against the glass, mentally willing the woman to move. Nothing happens. Blinking back tears, she raps hard on the glass. One at a time, the clocks fall silent. The cold window chills her face. She rocks back on her heels, out of ideas. How can she help the woman lying inches away, on the other side of the window?

"9-1-1!" she yelps, jumping to her feet. A man is walking right past the window, briefcase in hand. He slows, noticing Esmeralda. Puzzled, he looks at her for a second, shrugs, and then steps around her.

"Don't leave!" Maxzyne shouts, knocking hard on the window. Startled, he stops. Maxzyne motions to him and points. She nods as he kneels beside the unconscious woman.

"Hey! Are you all right?" The man gives Esmeralda a gentle shake. There is no response. Alarmed, the stranger looks at Maxzyne.

"What's wrong with her?" he shouts through the window. "Drugs? Alcohol?"

"Please, Mister, call an ambulance!"

Shrugging, the man reaches into his pocket for a cell phone. Maxzyne chews the end of a braid as he makes the call. Finally, the stranger stands, pointing east down Randolph Street.

"Ambulance is on its way!" With a wave of his briefcase, the man rushes off. Maxzyne's heart sinks until she hears a siren heading in her direction. Relieved, she calls to Esmeralda through the glass.

"They're coming to help you, Esmeralda. Don't worry. You'll be all right now."

"Don't worry, they're coming for you, all right!" sneers a familiar male voice behind her. "So this is where you've been hiding—in plain sight!"

Gasping, Maxzyne sees Jameson reflected behind her in the plate glass window. Clutching the heavy curtain in his brawny fist, he smirks.

"Where's your partner in crime?" he demands. His eyes flick about the small space. "Off hiding the loot, I suppose." He pays no attention to the mannequins. Maxzyne realizes he doesn't recognize Elise.

"We—I—I wasn't stealing." She clears her throat, trying to keep her voice from trembling. "I just needed to borrow some stuff—to help some-some friends." She trails off, knowing how silly she sounds.

"Yeah? Tell it to the police, little lady. They'll have you in handcuffs so fast your head will spin!" He points at her accusingly. "You kids are all the same—no respect for the law or adults!"

Jameson strides toward her. He leans forward, arms outstretched and ready to pounce. Maxzyne cringes against the cold glass. This time, there is no escape. Outside, the shrieking ambulance siren echoes off and around the nearby skyscrapers. Its insistent wail grows louder as it makes its way down Randolph Street toward them.

"Maybe that's the cops coming for you now, Missy. I never thought to look here. What're you doing by that window, anyway—trying to signal your gang? Get away from there!"

With a high-pitched squeal, Maxzyne kicks the golden egg near her foot. She feels it connect. The egg flies hard and straight into Jameson's looming face. "Score!" she yells.

Diving under the nearby table, she escapes while he is distracted and off balance. Heart pounding, she wriggles through table legs and then stands and topples the table in his direction.

"Why, you little—." There is a dull thud as the table hits the floor and another crash as Jameson trips over one of the table legs. Doing a belly flop, he lands on the Easter basket and crushes the contents.

"S-s-sorry!" she shrieks, darting through the curtain. Flying past the pile of clocks, she sways around the Japanese maple. Footsteps pound the floor behind her. Already Jameson has recovered and is after her. *What now?* Maxzyne skitters around the wet floor by the fountain that has not yet been mopped. "Over here! I'm over here," she teases. She ducks down behind the forsythia display.

Seconds later, Jameson slips on the wet floor. He crashes into the wall of flowers around the fountain's edge.

"Gotcha!" she whispers, knowing the flowers cushioned his fall.

"I'm going to have you locked up and throw away the key when I catch you!" Jameson shrieks. He rises to his knees. "Where are my handcuffs?" He scrabbles through the flowers, panting.

Handcuffs! Jail! Her stomach lurches. *No way! I am so out of here,* she thinks. *This adventure is out of control. I belong at home. With Mother and Dad.* Maxzyne rises from her hiding place. She makes a beeline for the cosmetics department and the hidden stairwell leading to the basement and the secret tunnel home.

Determined to catch her, Jameson follows. However, it sounds like he might be limping. "I'm going to crucify you for this! You're going to jail! I don't care how old you are! You'll rot there once I catch you!" he pants.

Maxzyne looks over the cosmetics department. With a thrill of joy, she recognizes the bronze screen that hides the old stairwell in the corner. It's the same one leading to the basement! But first, she'd better trick Jameson. No way he can follow her escape route.

With a quick turn, she runs past the Glam Diva Maquillage counter. Barbara is sitting there behind a mirrored cabinet. She is tallying up the daily sales. At the sound of Maxzyne's footsteps, she pauses, turning. Lifting her rhinestone-studded reading glasses, the woman calls out.

"Mr. Tracy? Is that you? I've almost got those numbers for you!" Hearing no response, she shrugs and returns the spectacles to her nose.

Maxzyne crouches behind a darkened glass counter. She kicks off her ankle boots, grabs

them by the buckles, and silently doubles back. She snakes between counters to the hidden stairs behind the screen. Finally, she ducks into the welcome darkness of the winding old staircase. Then she stops to listen.

"Jameson! What happened?" Barbara's voice rises in sympathy. "Why, you poor, poor, poor thing, you're all wet! Here, I've got some tissues right here. Let me help you—"

"Where'd she go? Did you see her—the little thief?" he sputters. "Well?" he demands. "Which way?"

Barbara clucks and coos, but he must be having none of it because she says more clearly, "Well, I didn't actually . . ." A groan from Jameson. "Let's see. I was working on my sales numbers for our spring promotion, sitting right over there, when I heard someone go that way, I suppose." Seconds later, she calls out, "Listen, are you sure you don't want me to—"

"All I want is that little criminal behind bars! Now!" Jameson's voice fades out. Maxzyne's double-back trick worked! Just like it did earlier for Peppin.

Her conscience pricks when she thinks of the mannequin family she's leaving behind. *No time for all that. Just get home!*

15

Chromatones

MAXZYNE RUNS DOWN the metal stairway. Her eyes slowly adjust to the gloom. Both red boots are tucked under her left arm. Her bare feet fly over the gritty, iron steps.

"Get me home!" she gasps, reaching the second to last landing. She turns, leaning over the rail, straining to see above her. There is no sign of Jameson. Can she find her way home? But what will she tell her parents? She frowns. They will never believe her crazy story about helping mannequins who . . . uh oh, there's her guilty conscience again. *What about Elise?* After all, Maxzyne promised to help the mannequin family. But now she's deserted them. Twisting a braid that has lost its barrette, she worries about not doing the right thing.

"What kind of hero dumps someone who needs help?" she asks out loud. "Oh, come on! They're just mannequins, silly!" She tosses the braid away from her face. "But Elise is like a sister now. Even if she is a mannequin." Maxzyne shakes her head. "Only a loser would leave now," she decides. "Nope, I have to go back." Turning around, Maxzyne puts one foot on the higher step. She anxiously looks back up the stairwell.

"But who will believe me now that they're all frozen again? Only Esmeralda." Maxzyne grips the banister with both hands, making her knuckles pale. She lets her chin rest on the railing. "She's too sick. And anyway, who would believe her? No one believes homeless people." She hunches over her clenched hands. But her ears prick, hearing a sudden rustle above her. Ready to run at the first sign of a door opening above, she waits in the dark. She holds her breath and listens. When nothing happens, she exhales. Then she opens her mouth and fills her lungs with musty air. *Breathe!*

Maxzyne swings the red suede boots, thinking out loud. "Justice-on-steroids Jameson? No way he'll ever believe me." She frowns, looking again at the top of the stairs. "Besides, I think he hates kids. Even if it wasn't his job, he'd probably still send me to jail." She sighs. "It *is* his job, and I'm going to jail." She turns around and jumps down a step, still trying to convince herself.

"And Mr. Tracy? He's hopping mad. He'll use my head to mop up the mess I made in his store BEFORE letting Jameson send me to jail forever!" Her mind made up, she races down the last few steps toward the basement, stirring up dust clouds. When she reaches the last step, she slaps her ankles and brushes the tops of her feet. "Mother will kill me if I get dirt on her silk carpet. And I'm *not* being a drama queen, believe me!" Turning around, Maxzyne looks once more up the darkened staircase. She anxiously bites her lip. It feels so wrong to run away from her promise.

"Up or down, clean or dirty, I'm busted," she declares. "So get over it, girl. Because right now you're going home. Even if Mother locks you up and throws away the key 'til you're eighteen." With a sigh, she sits down on the last step and pulls on the red suede boots. Her fingers smudge the soft leather.

"But Elise and the Frenches need me! I'm all they've got. So if I don't help, what's going to happen to them?" She leans on her knees, thinking hard. "If only there were some way I could convince Gigi not to . . . not to do anything to their . . ." Maxzyne gulps. Her hands move to her own neck.

"No way. Not me." Shaking her head, she stands. "Even if I tell her I want to be an artist someday, she'll just laugh and say I'm a kid who makes stuff up." She taps the iron railing. "Okay. I do make stuff up! But not this time! Seriously, people. This time it really happened."

Maxzyne turns away from the stairs. She tries not to think about the consequences of her actions. "I'm sorry, Elise . . ." she says softly.

Alone in the dark, Maxzyne shivers. She feels goose bumps rise on her arms and neck. *Is that a draft?* Without Elise and Peppin down here with her, everything is so much . . . scarier. *Were those shadows here before?* Maxzyne shivers again. She rubs the goose bumps on her arms. She eyes the eerie shapes in the shadowy gloom. Piles of odds and ends, years of store display items stacked up along the walls tower over her head. *Breathe!* She fills her lungs with dusty air.

But the shapes still seem menacing, as if they were getting closer, trying to squeeze her, smother her. Her heart thumps, making her gasp, as if the air were too thin. Out of the corner of her eye, she spots the old silver birdcage over by the cutting table. *If only Peppin were here to bark at those horrible stuffed parakeets with their staring, beady eyes!* She sticks her tongue out at them. "Can't scare me, ugly birds!" *Wait. Was that a rustling noise? Over . . . there?* "Okay, I'm out of here!" She darts past the birdcage and around the cutting table. A pair of oversized shears catches her eye. Perfect.

Warrior position! she breathes silently. Maxzyne listens hard, holding her yoga position. She slowly turns, scissors held high. There is nothing but a hodgepodge of wire hangers, baskets, frames, assorted stuffed animals, and an ancient sewing machine.

"Just some stupid mouse," Maxzyne decides.

She relaxes her grip on the shears. Then she strides through the clutter. She's puzzled when she can't find the door leading back to the tunnel and the condo freight elevator.

"Come on. It was around here somewhere. I know it was." Hands on hips, she tries to get her bearings. She steps over a pair of lace-up ice skates. "I remember these skates." Hearing a noise, this time to her left, she raises the scissors, ready to strike.

"Who—who's there? I know you're there! Come out!" Is someone behind her? Whipping around, she hears a scraping and shuffling noise. Where? To the right? The floor moves as the strange sound grows louder around her.

"Who are you? What do you want?" She shivers, but her hands sweat. This makes the shears hard to hold. Crouching down, she raises the shears toward the noise. "Come on! I'm not scared of—"

Choking on her words, she shrieks in terror. The shadows are moving! She can't believe her eyes. Tall, blank-faced figures walk stiffly. They are heading right for her! Their shuffling feet crush boxes. The robot figures leave broken odds and ends everywhere. Maxzyne's skin crawls as she watches the frightening figures.

"Chromatones!" she gasps, recalling the shadows she had pointed out to Elise earlier. Shrinking backwards, Maxzyne is trapped by the metal edge of

the cutting table. She clenches the shears with both hands. However, the slick handles slide in her grip as the monster forms keep coming toward her.

"Get back! Leave me alone!" she shrieks, twisting and turning. "Go away! You're not real! You don't even have faces." She waves her weapon. With a desperate lunge, she swings at the nearest one. She hits the blank-faced creature on the chest.

"Take that—you, you creepy Chromatone!" she yells. Too late, she realizes it is only a glancing blow. The heavy blade skitters across smooth, hard plastic until it finds softer material and makes a long tear. Maxzyne stares into the shiny, blank face of the robotic form. Its arm moves jerkily upward, knocking the shears from her hand. "Get away! Get away from me!" she cries. Caught in a crowd of Chromatones, she coughs, nearly choking. They smell like the inside of a plastic container left too long in the dishwasher. "I said leave me alone!" she sobs, trying to fend them off. Fists and elbows swinging, she struggles to keep her balance. "Help! Somebody!"

Maxzyne turns and crawls onto the cutting table. She slowly stands, watching the Chromatones' confusion as they reach for her but only bump into the table. She claps her hands when two of them crash into each other. However, she stops when they reach toward her with their grasping, plastic hands. "Help! Help me! Somebody! You've got to stop them!"

Maxzyne's shouts echo uselessly off the walls of the dim chamber. The table under her feet wobbles as bolts of fabric tumble from the shelves around her. "Warrior position!" she shouts, steadying herself as two Chromatones swipe at her. Desperate, she reaches for the birdcage swinging crazily on its stand. She throws it harder than she ever thought possible. The cage takes the crashing Chromatones by surprise, making the first row fall backward into the crowd of others.

Taking advantage of the confusion, Maxzyne grabs

a roll of cloth from the table. Quickly unwinding it, she flings it over the crowd of Chromatones nearest the table. Caught under the fabric, the hulking monsters fall. They send the next wave of creatures to the floor like falling dominoes. Now's her chance! Maxzyne leaps over the heaving mass. She lands on a nearby stack of empty hatboxes. The cardboard collapses under her weight. However, it breaks her fall, so she's not hurt. Maxzyne jumps up like a jack-in-a-box from the shredded layers of cardboard. She runs for her life toward the old iron stairs.

Her teeth chatter and her feet clatter up the metal steps. At the top of the first landing, she shrieks into the dark. "Esmeralda! Elise! Wha-what's going on?"

16

Think Positive

"STICK TO WHAT you know." Under her breath, Maxzyne repeats her father's advice over and over as she scurries through the huge, empty store. She knows she needs to get back to the display window where she left Elise and her family. She also knows how to get there without being seen. Maxzyne tiptoes past the cosmetics department. Barbara is still sitting at the counter. She is sorting through a stack of papers. Straight ahead are the fountain and the flower display Maxzyne hid behind earlier, with Elise and then alone.

Thinking of Elise, she begins to worry. What has happened to Esmeralda? Why are the mannequins no longer real? Why did the Chromatones come after her? Are these things connected? "*You don't know anything 'til you see for yourself*," she imagines her dad saying as she creeps through the store. But one worry replaces another. How will she explain her running away to Elise?

It's a perfectly normal thing to ask, Maxzyne thinks. *And Elise has every right to be mad that I left.* She pauses behind a pillar to catch her breath. Oh, what's normal about mannequins talking and walking? Or a poodle who talks? In French? Or mannequins needing my help to keep their heads from being used in some art exhibit? And what's normal about me thinking I can save them from being chopped up? Or convince Gigi that the mannequins are real? She tugs a braid near her cheek, bringing it to her mouth. She chews distractedly. It is several seconds before she realizes what she's doing.

"Pfffft!" How disgusting. She stopped chewing her braids in kindergarten!

"Okay. Just stick with the plan. Get to the window." Maxzyne slips past the tree and the fountain. She makes her way toward the white curtain. "Think positive," she breathes. "Nobody's chasing me. So that's positive."

Maxzyne rushes toward the white curtain. She grows more confident when there is still no sign of Jameson, Gigi, or Mr. Tracy. To her left, the clocks are still piled in a jumble from earlier. Before pulling aside the heavy drape, she suddenly freezes. What's this? Several boxes of new goods are neatly stacked beside an old metal work cart. "Oh, no!" she whispers.

Is she too late? Her knees suddenly buckle. She

begins to shake. Gift baskets of perfumed lotions, boxes of Crowne chocolates, piggy banks, kitchen utensils, aprons, placemats, napkins, tablecloths, and glassware wait for display in the window. And there's her tote bag! She reaches down to pick it up. To her relief, Faith, her doll, is safely tucked away. The painting of Peppin, her swim cap, and her goggles are also there. Maxzyne feels better just putting the bag on her shoulder. With ears on high alert, she tiptoes toward the curtain. Then slowly, carefully, she draws it back and peeks in.

17

Window Dressing

"ELISE? ARE YOU THERE?" Silence. Maxzyne whispers louder, "Elise! Peppin?" Still no answer. *Think positive,* she reminds herself. Ever so carefully, she slips through the familiar opening. But she is suddenly blinded by glaring, overhead spotlights. She gasps. The once-cheerful window has been stripped of all decorations. If it weren't for the glass in front of her, she could be standing in an empty box. Worse, the mannequins have been pushed into a corner. They are stacked neatly against one another, from Peppin, the smallest, to Aloin, the largest. His chin is tucked into Veronique's mussed hair. It is heartbreaking to see that even in these awkward positions, their backs are straight and they still seem proud and dignified.

"Oh, Elise," Maxzyne breathes. "At least they left your clothes on! Gigi must be getting ready to take you away to—!"

She runs to look out the window, hoping to find Esmeralda. But the only sign of her is the battered suitcase. It is still sitting next to the window. Tears prick Maxzyne's eyes.

"Stop it!" she scolds herself. "I'm Maxzyne 'the Greatest' Merriweather. There must be something I can do!" She stamps her heel, hands on hips. "Well, they're stuck with me now! This time, I'm waiting for Gigi. I'm just going to face her. I'll tell her that if she tries cutting anything . . . anybody . . . any of my friends, I'm going to, well, I'll make *her* into a sculpture and see how she likes it!"

Maxzyne wipes her eyes with the sleeve of her denim jacket. She strides back to the mannequin family. "And you don't have to be stuck together like old paper dolls, either. Here. I know you'd rather have a view," she says to Elise. She pushes her to the window and leans her against the glass. "Good. Now you can see people and make up stories about them. Right?"

Maxzyne runs back to the corner. She returns with Peppin in her arms. Then she carefully sets the poodle down beside Elise. "And here's Peppin. He likes to hear your stories. Remember?" She softly strokes the poodle's ears. Maxzyne surveys the two figures now positioned by the window. She frowns, casting a critical eye.

"Nope. You can't see if your hair's messed up. Can you?" Maxzyne brushes Elise's blonde hair away from her eyes. She skillfully weaves two small braids on either side of the still, white face. Then she carefully pulls back the braids and secures them with one of her own barrettes. Smiling, she raises her hand, offering a fist bump. But Elise's arm remains frozen by her side. Dropping her hand, Maxzyne bows her head. She cannot look Elise in the eye.

"Elise . . . please don't be mad . . . I didn't mean to leave. I just didn't know what to do when Jameson came after me like that! You must have seen him. He said I was going to jail! So, okay, I freaked! I know I said I'd save you guys. But when it was just me . . .

and then Esmeralda was . . ."

Maxzyne swallows hard and looks up at Elise. She tries to smile, but her bottom lip quivers. "Elise, do you think Esmeralda will get better? Will she come back, so everything will be normal again?" She looks out at the suitcase abandoned on the sidewalk. "I know. What is *normal,* right? But you know what I mean. Will you ever be real again? And your parents and Peppin? Anyway, I'm sorry I ran. Some kind of hero, me, thinking I could save everybody, huh?"

The blonde mannequin remains quiet and still. Maxzyne sighs. She shrugs out of her jacket, placing it on the floor. "Well, while we're waiting for Gigi, I might as well tell the first story." Her back to the window, she easily drops into a seated position. She hugs her knees.

"You'll never believe what happened!" Maxzyne looks at Peppin and Elise. Then she recalls her scary adventure in the store basement. *Breathe.* She sighs again. Then she leans back against the window, ready to start. "Remember those Chromatones? No, wait, I'll get to that. Okay . . . from the top."

"So, I'm crossing the main floor, trying to find that old staircase we came up. But I hear Jameson coming after me. So I run, right? Well, I don't have time to think about where to hide. But somehow I end up heading toward cosmetics. Remember where that Barbara lady painted our faces and then sprayed us with that stinky perfume?" Maxzyne pauses to sniff her arm. Then she makes a face. "Anyway, that's when I see the screen that's in front of the old staircase!" She grins at Peppin and Elise.

"Anyway, before I can get there, I have to go past the fountain. But Jameson, he's getting so close I know any second I'll be dead, er, I mean, caught." She grips her knees, shaking her head. "And I'm already running as fast as I can! But then I remember that it's all wet by the fountain and really slippery from when Mr. Tracy tried to catch Peppin. Remember, Peppin?" Maxzyne gives the dog a little pat. "So I lead Jameson right there. And sure enough, he slips and wipes out, totally! Crash! Bam! A belly flop right into the flowers. Meanwhile, I duck around the other side of the fountain and never look back." Maxzyne chuckles. She stops to stroke Peppin's nose. "Thanks to you and Mr. Tracy's little splash earlier." She buries her face in the poodle's fur.

"So next, I hide behind a counter near where Barbara, the cosmetics lady, works. But I take off my boots because they're way too loud on the marble floor. Just in time 'cause I hear Jameson again! Now he's really, really mad. He's yelling like crazy, saying he's going to put me in jail, stuff like that. Hey! Do kids really go to jail?" Unable to decide, she shrugs.

"Anyway, I'm not sticking around to get caught. So I run past the cosmetics counter, making lots of noise.

Then I double back on tiptoe. Just like Peppin did to throw Tracy and Jameson off our trail, Elise." Maxzyne pauses, remembering.

"So the double-back trick must have worked because from the stairs I hear Barbara sending Jameson off in the exact wrong direction! Still, I run like crazy, just in case! Finally, at the bottom of the stairs, since no one followed me, I figure I'm safe."

Maxzyne shifts position. She tucks her legs to one side. "But once I'm down there in the dark by myself, well, I . . . Don't be mad, Elise, but I start thinking, you know, maybe I should just go home. I mean, okay, I *want* to go home. I'll just follow those daisies you dropped and find the secret tunnel to the freight elevator. And then, well, back home." She hangs her head. Her face flushes as she rubs the buckle on one ankle boot with her denim sleeve.

"It's true . . . I just gave up. I mean, who am I going to save, except me? Guess you didn't know Maxzyne Merriweather was all imagination and no guts, did you? Plus, I thought, well, maybe Mother wouldn't be so angry, wouldn't punish me . . . at least when she saw I was okay. Maybe she'd even be happy." She chews her bottom lip, frowning. "Well, probably I *will* get grounded for life. But that's better than jail. Right?" Maxzyne looks to Elise and Peppin for agreement, but they remain silent. "Yeah, well, maybe it's the same thing, really. Funny, you never once complained about being stuck in a window, Elise."

Maxzyne stretches her legs again. She knocks the toes of her boots together. "Don't say it! I know what you're thinking." She sighs, hands upturned. "You're right. All talk, no action, and always complaining I never get to do stuff. That's me." Frowning, she continues.

"But listen to this. Before I can find the door that leads back to the secret tunnel, something really weird happens. I mean, I still can't believe it. Remember the Chromatones? Those faceless freak mannequins? I swear, they came alive and started chasing me! It was the scariest thing ever! They're horrible. Like giant evil robots. They trapped me! So I grabbed some big scissors and started swinging. I almost stabbed one, but they wouldn't stop! Don't even ask how I got away, but I did." Shuddering, she takes Elise's hand.

"Anyway, I just have this feeling that somehow it's all happening this way because of Esmeralda, Elise. I mean, it seems like she's got some kind of power or something. Doesn't it? Because you were real until she got sick and fainted. All I know is, when those Chromatones started coming after me, I thought maybe her powers or her magic—something had gone crazy!"

Maxzyne fingers the gold chain around her neck, thinking, *I just don't know. But I wish she'd come back.*

18

Esmeralda

FROM BEHIND MAXZYNE, on the other side of the glass, there is a sudden loud rapping and a raspy voice calls out, "Oh, child, you do know how to tell some kind of story, that's for sure! Old Esmeralda, she doesn't have that kind of power, girl. No magic!" She laughs, rocking back and forth. "Oh, my, magic powers!"

"Esmeralda! How long have you been there? Are you okay?"

"Oh, I've been listening for quite a time." She chuckles again.

"We were so scared when you, when you fainted. I tried everything to wake you up, but then a man came along and called an ambulance."

"You are a good child, even if you do tell tall tales!" The woman's eyes twinkle, and she gives Maxzyne a gap-toothed grin. Then her face grows dark. "It was that candy. You know, those doctors, the medical folks, they always telling me, 'Esmeralda, no sweets! No candy.' Well, you tell me how I'm going to say no when some nice folks give me chocolate? Could you?"

Maxzyne shakes her head.

Nodding, Esmeralda continues. "And I only ate a few bites. Those doctors, they say, you've got to take these pills every day, Esmeralda, so you won't get sick and pass out. But, you know, I've got no use for pills. I've got no use for them at all. Never have, never will. I wasn't raised with pills, and I won't take them. I just live my life, and what happens is just meant to be."

Frowning, she takes two plastic bottles of capsules out of her coat pocket. She holds them up to the glass. "Pills? Can't trust them!" Unscrewing the lids, she walks to the curb and dumps the contents, spraying the red and blue pills into the street where they bounce and roll into the gutter. Returning the empty bottles to her pockets, she throws her hood up over her hair, letting out a satisfied shriek. "Aiiiiieeee!!"

Maxzyne jumps to her feet, pounding on the glass. "Esmeralda, that's your medicine! You can't just throw it out! You're supposed to take it!"

The woman shakes her head. "No! Can't trust them!" She stomps on the pills, crushing them with her worn black shoes.

"Stop! You'll get sick again! You don't want to be sick, do you?"

Esmeralda stalks back to the window, smiling at Peppin and Elise. She looks puzzled to see Aloin and Veronique pushed in the corner. She points angrily. "What did you do to my friends, girl? Where are their voices?"

Maxzyne is confused. "But I thought you were the one who—? Weren't you?" Esmeralda stands with her hands on her hips, shaking her head. Maxzyne stares at Esmeralda. "You made them real, didn't you? It was something you did, making them talk and everything, right? I mean, you were talking to them when Mother and I saw you this afternoon. You gave me Peppin's picture, remember?"

Esmeralda sits down on her suitcase with a thump, yawning. Her breath frosts the glass with a cloudy haze. Using the tip of a crooked, nail-bitten finger, she draws several eyes on the glass.

"Well, if it wasn't you," Maxzyne begs, "who was it?"

"I told you, I don't make magic! That's your own crazy story, girl. It's from your own head, so don't put it on me," the woman answers, clearing the eye images with an angry sweep of her ragged coat sleeve. "Everybody's always telling me what I did, when I didn't."

"Okay, okay. I'm sorry, Esmeralda." Maxzyne kneels, pulling Peppin closer to the window so his nose rests against the glass. Clapping her hands,

Esmeralda jumps to her feet and unzips the battered suitcase.

"Pretty boy. Pretty boy," she coos. She takes a stack of paintings out of her bag and holds one up for Maxzyne to see. It is another picture of Peppin, this one without polka dots or a fancy collar.

"Peppin! Before they gave him polka dots?" Maxzyne smiles, stroking the poodle beside her.

The woman nods, fanning out the stack in her hands. There are paintings of Elise by herself and others showing her with Aloin and Veronique. There are sketches of pigeons, the accordion musician, even the Tina Turner look-alike street performer in her black fringed dress and shiny gold heels. Finally, there's a sketch of the tiny fountain on Garland Court, the building Maxzyne lives in, showing a homeless man washing his shirt. Esmeralda nods proudly, before returning the dog-eared paintings to her suitcase. Then she pulls an artist's sketchbook and a small box of colored pastels out of another compartment.

"Hey, I've got some just like that!" Maxzyne says, pointing to them. "Mother got them for me at Blick's art store down the street."

Esmeralda silently zips her suitcase closed. Standing it upright on the sidewalk, she again uses it as a seat. Holding the sketch pad on her knees, she looks calmly at Maxzyne and begins to sketch. The young girl sees her own face and braids take shape beneath the woman's bony fingers, the smallest one crooked and pointing at an odd angle. Trying hard not to move, Maxzyne finally breaks Esmeralda's concentration.

"What happened to your finger, Esmeralda?"

Esmeralda shrugs and continues to make bold lines on the blank page, choosing her colors carefully. Maxzyne strains to see the sketch.

"Where'd you learn to draw like that, Esmeralda?"

The woman snorts, sucking in her cheeks. Finally, she chooses a deep violet shade from the box. Maxzyne recognizes one of her barrettes taking shape on the paper and self-consciously checks her braids. Absorbed in her art, Esmeralda is silent. Finally, she speaks, as if from some faraway place. "Esmeralda, she loves colors. Mama bought me a box, long time ago, when I was a girl like you. I used to draw on newspapers she brought home from the big houses she'd clean."

Using the edge of her crooked finger to smudge the bold strokes of Maxzyne's cheekbones and brows, she frowns. "My brothers and me, we didn't have toys. Only thing we had a lot of was nothing. So when I got my colors, my brothers were jealous. They didn't like me having fun and coloring and drawing. It took my mama's eyes away from them, I guess.

"One day I came in from doing my chores and those boys had melted all my crayons on the stove, they had. I could have killed them, but of course I didn't. Just went out back and cried about it. Just our old dog, the rooster, and a bunch of chickens to hear me. Mama whipped those boys and scolded them when she got home, but mostly because they ruined her good gravy pan. And then she whipped me for not watching them better."

"I didn't know brothers could be so mean!" Maxzyne sits up straight, horrified. "I always wanted a brother, but maybe I'm glad I never got one."

"Oh, they were just being boys, child. We all took our whippings."

"But your mother . . . well, she, she whipped you?" Maxzyne gulps.

Esmeralda nods her head, continuing to sketch. "That's the way they do sometimes. Said it would get my attention."

"Not my parents. When I do something wrong, they make me learn a new multi-syllable word. Spelling and definition. Like 'minimalism.'" As the syllables roll off her tongue, she counts, using her fingers. "A style or technique characterized by extreme spareness and simplicity," she recites. "How's that?"

But Esmeralda ignores Maxzyne. She concentrates on her drawing, carefully choosing just the right color to shade the girl's cheeks. "Those boys . . . they were plenty of trouble, but fun, too, when they wanted. I guess I loved them, no matter what they got up to. It was work, though, keeping up with them and doing my chores. I was worn out most times."

"Didn't you go to school?"

"School?" Esmeralda cackles. "I learnt how to spell my name in Sunday school, and that's all the learning there was for me, girl. 'No time for it,' Mama said, 'with so many mouths to feed.'" With a critical eye, she gazes at Maxzyne's throat, pointing at the partially hidden gold chain.

"What's that sparkler you're hiding there?"

Maxzyne's hand flies to her throat. She lifts the fine gold chain to show Esmeralda her pendant.

"My dad got it for me in Switzerland. It's a baby bell—like cows wear so they don't get lost." She shakes the bell, making it jingle merrily.

"Hoo, hoo, sparklers for cows!" Esmeralda cackles again, ending with a coughing fit. "So they don' get lost, huh? Oh, that's a good one! Your stories! I sure do like them!" Then her face grows serious. "Are you

wearing that so you don't get lost, child?"

"No! I live right over . . . there!" Maxzyne points right down Randolph Street. "In the building at the next corner. You saw me outside this afternoon with Mother—that's when you gave me the painting, remember?"

"You say I—I did?" The woman struggles to remember. Leaning forward on the glass, she suddenly smiles. "That was you? Gave me . . . I know!" She goes through her coat pockets, spilling bottle caps, twist ties, pencil nubs, matchbooks, several coins, and a bruised daffodil blossom. Finally, she waves several dollar bills.

"Yes! I gave you those for the picture you gave me of Peppin!" Maxzyne puts her arm around the poodle, nodding. Esmeralda stuffs the bills and other items back into her cloak.

"You made the voices," she mutters, pointing at Maxzyne.

"What do you mean? I didn't do anything. I just gave you the money I saved for my doll's next outfit or game app to download on Mother's computer."

"The voices came when you gave the money, child."

Maxzyne stares at the woman in disbelief.

"You mean the mannequins came alive because I gave you money?" she gasps. "Well, what are we waiting for? If all I have to do is—"

She jumps to her feet and races across the window to get her tote bag. Removing Faith, she dumps it upside down, throwing her swim cap, goggles, and Faith's art tools aside. Her slim fingers search the inside pocket. Empty. She returns to the window, head hanging. "I don't have any money with me," she says sadly. "Isn't there another way to wake them up? Please, Esmeralda!"

"Not for me to say, child. But you can have this one, if you want." Esmeralda holds up the finished picture of Maxzyne, smiling again through gapped teeth.

"Thanks, but all I want is to wake my friends up and keep Gigi from cutting off their heads." Maxzyne brushes Elise's throat, letting her hand rest on the mannequin's shoulder. "Isn't there something you can do?"

Standing, Esmeralda shakes her head. "Esmeralda can't do magic, I told you! Now get on home. Your mama's waiting, don't you know?"

"Yes . . . but I can't just leave them, Esmeralda! Elise is my friend now, and I—well, I want them to be safe!"

Esmeralda stands up, chuckling. "Safe? Don't you worry yourself about them being safe now! I'll be right here with them. Watching out. Now you go on home!"

Maxzyne looks sheepish. "Well . . . the truth is, I can't go home. I promised to stay here until Jameson, Mr. Tracy, or Gigi finds me. Whoever it is will be really mad, because I made a mess when me and Elise were in the store earlier."

She sighs, turning to the still figure beside her. "But we had fun, didn't we, Elise?" Nodding, Maxzyne continues. "I made her a birthday party. Did you know she's eleven now, Esmeralda?" She suddenly lifts the gold chain from around her own neck and struggles with the dainty clasp. Finally succeeding, she turns and fastens the necklace around Elise's smooth throat.

"Now that's a nice thing to do for your girl," Esmeralda says. "Your mama, she taught you right, didn't she?"

"What do you mean?"

"You learned to share. Out here on the street, don't see so much sharing going on." Esmeralda rises, hands on hips, surveying the evening street. "Nope. Thing is, I didn't know I'd be needing people to share when I left home just a girl." She sits slowly down on the suitcase, her high forehead wrinkling as she remembers.

"You mean you ran away?"

"I surely did, child. When I was growing up, I had to share everything—even the bath—with my brothers. I was last, so there was only dirty water and the ring to clean, too. Well, now, one of the Johnson boys, farmers down on Creek Road, came calling round to see me one Sunday and told me how good life was in the big city. Said how if I came away with him, up here to Chicago, I'd have myself a real good time. Yes, indeed!" Esmeralda slaps her knee. "No more chores all day, nobody telling me all the time what to do and when to do it! Just me and Jimmy."

"So you went with him? What happened?"

"Of course I went. I'm here, aren't I?" Eyebrows rising in dark peaks, she looks hard at Maxzyne, who nods.

"Well, the city grew me up fast, child. Too fast. Jimmy and me, we were just kids when we got here. Jimmy tried, but he didn't know much except farm work. He did odd jobs, but, well, after a while we had a little one coming, and what money we had Jimmy used to spend on lottery tickets and schemes that never amounted to much. Finally fell in with some bad company and just disappeared one day. Don't know what happened, but I never saw him again. Poor Jimmy. He wasn't a bad man, just a farm boy, over his head in the big city. Like me. And like my mama did, I cleaned houses for rich folks. I was too proud to go back home." Esmeralda sighs, shaking her head, looking at her empty hands.

"My son was born with my same crooked finger, too." She tugs at her bent finger sadly. "My boy, Jeffrey?" She smiles, looking thoughtful. "Such a sweet baby. But after awhile, I just couldn't keep my boy and a job, too. It broke my heart when I gave him up. Those people at Social Services took him. Said he'd have a better life than what I could give."

Esmeralda turns away, glancing up and down the evening street. Maxzyne thinks of all the families out there, in their houses and apartments, eating their dinners and getting ready for bed. Families in all shapes, sizes, and conditions. And somewhere out there is Esmeralda's son.

"Think he misses his mama?" Esmeralda asks, turning back. "No." She answers her own question. "Probably not. He doesn't even remember."

Tears spring to Maxzyne's eyes. What can she say when her own mother must be going crazy with worry? Esmeralda gets up suddenly, rising to smash a plastic cup abandoned on the sidewalk.

"Too many folks use these cups for begging," she mutters. "Just because you're down, living on the street, doesn't mean you just get a handout. Sure, some people have hard times, but begging? Kills your pride, that's what. Me? I sell my paintings. Nobody can say Esmeralda doesn't earn her keep! And when I get paid, I don't mind sharing. Even with the pigeons," she exclaims, flinging her arms out wide and scaring two perched on a nearby lamp post. She points at Maxzyne, her voice serious.

"But, girl, you've got a home. Makes no sense you growing up fast like me. You take your time; let the years come to you. They'll find you, those years will. Oh, yes . . . they'll find you . . ." Esmeralda shivers, clutching the folds of her red cloak closer to her body.

"But what about Elise and Peppin? They were real, weren't they? We can still save them, right?"

Esmeralda leans close again, her nose smudging the glass. She looks Maxzyne straight in the eye.

"Everybody's 'real' is different, child. Me? I see with my eyes, but I paint with my heart. Understand?" Maxzyne nods, lost in thought. "Never mind what's real. You just take your dreams and make them real, missy."

Esmeralda places her palm on the glass, and Maxzyne puts her own smaller hand against it on the other side. Behind Esmeralda, a blue-and-yellow, striped taxi cruises past the window. The street lamp lights the familiar face of a man in the back seat. "Dad!" she cries out, her hands smacking the glass. "Esmeralda, that's my dad! Daddy! Over here!" She jumps up and down, waving her arms. "Quick, Esmeralda! Get him for me!" Turning, she is puzzled when the woman is no longer there. Across the street, a figure rolling a suitcase quickly blends into the shadows.

"Don't leave, Esmeralda! It's okay!"

Maxzyne watches the taxi slow at the intersection of State Street. Still hopeful, she raps hard on the glass, bruising her knuckles.

"Dad! Over here! It's me!"

Did he hear me? When the light turns green, her heart lurches as the taxi glides around the corner, speeds up, and is quickly out of sight.

19

Face-to-Face

MAXZYNE CRUMPLES to the floor. Tears leak from the corners of her eyes, and she pulls her denim jacket over her face, ashamed to cry in front of the staring mannequins. For several minutes she lies there, sobbing quietly. If only her father had seen her. Now what? From under her jacket, she hears the swish of the heavy white curtain as it is drawn aside.

"Soon as we get these windows set up, do you mind if I borrow your cart, Ray?" asks a familiar voice.

"Gigi," Maxzyne whispers. Bolting upright, she flings the jacket from her face, quickly wiping her eyes. Well, at least the waiting is over. She'll have to face the music for the trouble she's caused, but maybe she can still save the mannequins.

"Sure, you can borrow it. Just be careful. Like me, it's a real antique!" Ray laughs.

"Hey, I've seen you climb ladders three stories tall,

decorating the Crowne Court Christmas tree," Gigi reminds him.

"Well, age before beauty then, my dear." Ray ducks his head and enters the small space. He holds the curtain aside for Gigi, giving a quick bow.

"Always the gentleman, Ray."

"Yep. Don't make them like me anymore. Old-time manners. Nothing wrong with a man being polite. You young people laugh, but I open doors for ladies, you know, and offer my arm if they need it." He pulls some of the fluffy, white cleaning towels out of her hands, stuffing them in his green work apron pockets.

"Those old-time manners sound perfect—for Ms. Mitchell." Gigi grins.

Maxzyne listens to their chatter, her back against the window. They haven't noticed her yet, but what's all this talk of being polite? Gigi, the one who's going to cut the heads off mannequins? Talking about manners?

Ray shakes his head at Gigi. "Not me. A man's got to know his limitations."

Gigi throws one of the cleaning towels at him. "C'mon. You know you two are perfect for each other."

"But she's no antique—she's a classic."

"And you have a classic case of nerves when it comes to asking her out on a date!"

Shrugging helplessly, Ray changes the subject. "What do you need my cart for, anyway?"

"For my mannequins, of course. Once they're

undressed, I've got to get them to my friend's truck."

Maxzyne gasps, imagining the mannequin family's distress at hearing this news. Ray and Gigi turn toward her, startled.

"Er, sorry," Maxzyne mumbles. "I, uh, sort of moved them." Her finger shaking, she points to Elise and Peppin. "So they could see better . . ."

"Uh oh." Ray points at her. "So you're the little tornado that's got the place in lockdown!" He peers at her through his thick glasses. "For such a small thing, you sure made a big mess in the Lollipop and Soda Shop," he says sternly. He looks around, perplexed. "But I heard there were two of you. Mr. Tracy's going nuts looking for you both right now."

"And what are you doing with my mannequins, you little worm? Get away from them—now!" Gigi glares at Maxzyne, her charcoal-rimmed eyes and red lips frightening in the glare of the floodlights. A dragon tattoo pulses around her pale neck, making its outstretched wings appear to move.

Maxzyne shrinks away to the far end of the window, but Gigi follows, eyes blazing. "I didn't mean it! I mean, I just wanted to—"

"Better call Jameson, Ray. Hate to make his day, but we need some law and order here. That is, if he can handle a minor."

"Okay. How old are you, anyway?" Ray asks. He pulls a phone out of his pocket.

"Ten."

Flicking her hair from her shoulder, Gigi stands in front of Maxzyne, arms crossed, silently daring her to move. She taps her black, stiletto boot impatiently.

"Please," Maxzyne says. "Please, you don't have to call him. Really, I can explain . . ."

Gigi glares down at her. Maxzyne's mouth goes dry. "Well? I'm listening . . ."

Desperately licking her lips, Maxzyne wonders where to begin.

"Going straight to voicemail," Ray interrupts. Maxzyne is grateful for the distraction.

"Hey, Jameson, Ray here. Give me a call. Think I found your little problem down here in the corner window—State and Randolph." Dropping the phone into his apron pocket, Ray gives Maxzyne a stern look. "So where's your partner in crime, miss? You know, the sooner you cooperate, the better it'll go for you both."

"She's . . . uh, she's . . . well, it doesn't matter." *Ray isn't as scary as Gigi,* she thinks, looking at his kind eyes. "You wouldn't believe me if I told you, sir." She looks at the floor, her braids falling across her face, hoping to hide from Gigi's glaring eyes.

Ray's voice softens. "Well, whoever she is, you're both pretty clever, I've got to say." He removes his glasses, using a towel to carefully wipe the lenses.

Gigi's brow arches. "How's that, Ray? Kids make a mess and more work for us, so you're handing out compliments?"

He returns the glasses to his nose, shrugging. "Hey, nobody's used that old dumbwaiter for years, much less to escape old Tracy. Wish I'd thought of it myself, sometimes." He grins in admiration. "What's your name, anyway?"

"Maxzyne. Maxzyne Merriweather."

Gigi steps close. "Well, Ms. Merriweather, I can't say you look familiar, but this must be an inside job, because how else would anyone know about that old dumbwaiter?" Maxzyne cringes, looking down at her blistered hands. Gigi pounces, grabbing her by the elbow. As she forces Maxzyne's palm face up, her almond eyes narrow, seeing the red rope-burn marks.

"Well, I . . . uh . . . live next door and shop here a lot with my—"

"Just got your message!" Jameson crows, bursting through the curtain. His eyes zero in on Maxzyne. "There you are, you little hoodlum! Back to the scene, eh? Yep, that's what they do, these criminals. They get cocky and they get greedy!"

Behind him, the curtain swishes. Uh oh. This time it's Mr. Tracy. "Caught the little troublemaker, did we?" Like Jameson, he is rumpled and damp, his neat bow tie at an angle. Recognizing Maxzyne, he strokes his mustache, looking smug. "I warned you! There's no place to hide that we couldn't catch you, Missy! And we did! Oh, yes. We got you." He nods at the security detective. "Nice work, Jameson."

Gigi looks at Ray and rolls her eyes before stepping forward. "Well, like I was saying, Ray. It seems it might have been an inside job. Nobody but an employee would know about the dumbwaiter, right?"

"Er, right, right." Ray tries to keep a straight face as he turns to the rumpled store manager. "Only old-timers like us would even know it existed, boss."

Jameson shakes his head, pointing at Maxzyne. "This one's no old-timer! And her little partner in crime is the same age! A little blonde girl—just ask Ms. Mitchell upstairs! We both saw her!" Jameson reaches into his pocket and takes out a pair of handcuffs. Smirking, he dangles them in front of Maxzyne. "These bracelets will make you talk . . ."

"Are those really necessary, Jameson?" Ray protests. "C'mon, she's just a kid."

"YES!" shriek both Mr. Tracy and the security detective. Gigi looks away, trying not to laugh.

Ignoring them, Ray kneels beside the scared girl. "Listen, Maxzyne. Nobody wants any trouble here. If you'll just tell us where we can find your friend, we can call both your parents and get this mess straightened out, okay?"

"Nice touch, Ray. Good cop, bad cop, huh?" Gigi rattles her silver skull-and-cross-bone chains impatiently.

With a gentle look, Ray places his hand on

Maxzyne's shoulder. "You believe me, don't you, Maxzyne?

She nods, swallowing hard.

"So tell me what's going on here. I'll believe you."

Taking a deep breath, Maxzyne points to Elise. Everyone turns and looks at the mannequin.

"Say what?" Gigi looks shocked. "Well, that's a new one! Blame it on the mannequins. My mannequins, I might add." She shoots an angry, doubtful look at Ray.

Mr. Tracy gives Jameson a nod. Smirking, the detective moves toward Maxzyne. "All right, enough fun and games, kid. If you don't want to talk to us, you're going down to the police station. Let's go."

"Owwwwwww!" she screams when he grabs her blistered hand.

"Don't hurt her, Jameson! She's not a criminal, she's a kid. You're scaring her to death." Ray scowls at the detective, who unwillingly pockets his handcuffs. "Keep going with your story, Maxzyne. I'm listening."

His kind eyes encourage Maxzyne to continue. "I know you're all mad. I can't blame you." She stands taller, hands tucked safely behind her back. "And, and I'm sorry about the mess I made. But you have to believe me—I never meant to be this much trouble." She looks at the ground. "The truth is, I'm in enough trouble with my mother already." Biting her bottom lip, she continues shakily. "But Elise she, well, they all needed my help—I wanted to save them somehow."

His arms crossed, Jameson shakes his head in disbelief. "You believe this, boss?" Mr. Tracy shrugs.

"Really, I did! It's just that I got distracted and Elise—"

"Who's Elise? That girl mannequin?" Gigi looks doubtful. "Nice touch, giving her a name, kid."

"But they all have names! Even Peppin, the poodle!"

"The only names I need are your parents'. Somebody's got to pay for your mess." Mr. Tracy rubs his mustache, frowning at his ruined pants.

"Calm down and let her speak, everyone!" Ray interrupts. Maxzyne smiles gratefully. "Go ahead, finish your story."

"Well, sir, I live in the building next door, see? Anyway, I snuck out for a swim because my mother was—well, never mind. Things got really crazy when I took the freight elevator, and I got stuck in the dark. Scary! I yelled, but nobody heard me."

Ray looks at Mr. Tracy, but the manager rolls his eyes, saying nothing.

"Anyway, the elevator kind of crashed and I got out, but I was all alone in this strange tunnel. That is, until Elise found me—and Peppin!" She points at the poodle. Jameson follows her gaze, scowling. She tries not to notice his fingers tapping the handcuffs sticking out of his pocket.

"Go on, finish your fairy tale," Mr. Tracy growls.

"So . . . Elise showed me the way to your store. You know, through the tunnel, into the basement, and then up the stairs. We pretended we were store models—the cosmetics ladies even made us up! Then Elise brought me here to meet her parents." She turns, pointing. "That's them—Aloin and Veronique. They're French." Everyone looks at the adult mannequins in the corner.

"Well, she's got a colorful imagination; I'll give her that, Ray." Scowling, Gigi walks over to smooth Veronique's mussed hair.

"I think you should pay attention to what

Maxzyne's telling us," Ray says. "Most folks don't even know those old tunnels exist. These mannequins were lost until we discovered that old storeroom down below. And it was only because of the flood! To be honest, I'd probably get lost trying to find my way down there again!" He chuckles, his kind eyes crinkling. "But why did Elise need your help?"

"Oh, yeah. I guess I forgot that part." Maxzyne hesitates, nervously licking her dry lips, afraid to look at Gigi.

"Well? The clock is ticking on this story . . ." The young woman's skull-and-crossbones chains jangle as she flicks her red-tipped hair over her shoulder.

"Elise needed help 'cause she said you were going to cut their heads off and make a sculpture out of them for some art exhibit."

Ray is impressed. "Bingo! She's right about that one, isn't she?"

"Don't be so easily fooled, Ray." The dragon tattoo pulses faster on Gigi's neck. "She probably just heard me talking about it and—"

Maxzyne suddenly pulls the origami paper bird from Elise's daisy-smocked pocket. Unfolding it, she holds it up for Ray to read aloud: "School of the Art Institute of Chicago announces 'HEAD CASE,' a contest that will exhibit—"

"Hey! Where'd you get that? Give it here!" Gigi snatches it out of Maxzyne's hand.

"Elise gave it to me. That's why I knew she needed help."

"Nice try, kid. But that story won't fly. Living mannequins? I don't *think* so."

"But you are using them for that exhibit, aren't you?" Ray argues.

"Just paid me for them tonight," Mr. Tracy states.

Ray rises, walking to stand near Elise. He checks her dress again, peering at the missing daisy trim; Maxzyne's barrette holding her hair; the scuffed, white Mary Jane shoes; and the pollen smudge on her arm. "Look at all this, Gigi. How do you explain it?"

"Oh, Ray! She just moved the mannequins around and messed them up. She can't fool me. And that flyer about the exhibit? I've been giving them out to everybody! Don't believe everything Little Ms. Big Imagination says."

Jameson chimes in. "Yeah, don't trust a word she says—she'll say anything to avoid the consequences."

"No! It's not like that!" Maxzyne tries to catch Ray's eye, but he's looking at Gigi.

He pushes his glasses higher on his nose, shrugging. "Well . . . I just hate to think that—"

"Please! You've got to believe me!" Desperate, Maxzyne pushes past Jameson to get her tote bag.

"Hey, don't even think about trying to get away!" Lurching forward, Mr. Tracy grabs Maxzyne's arm.

"I'm not running away. Promise. I just want

to show you something." Grunting, the manager unwillingly drops her arm. Maxzyne tips the bag upside down, letting the contents spill onto the floor. "Sorry, Faith." Picking up the doll, she hugs her to her chest.

Jameson points at the navy swimsuit. "Hey, that suit's one of ours—I saw it upstairs earlier." Hands on hips, he looks at the store manager. "Ask Ms. Mitchell—she'll ID it."

"I know. My mother bought it for me this afternoon. I told you I was going to the pool." She goes through the items on the floor. "Look—here's what I want to show you!" She picks up Esmeralda's picture of Peppin and waves it at her audience. "I sort of forgot the most important part of the story," she explains. "I know this sounds weird, but Esmeralda, this homeless woman, she gave me this painting, and when I—"

"Let me see that!" Gigi snatches the picture from Maxzyne. Her eyes narrow when she sees the signature in the corner. "Esmeralda gave you this?"

"Yes, when I was standing outside the window earlier this afternoon."

Ray looks confused. "Gigi, who is Esmeralda? Not that poor homeless woman who's always talking to herself out there?" He jerks a thumb toward the street.

"That's the last thing we need hanging around our windows, scaring customers away! Hear that Jameson? You're supposed to be my eyes and ears!" Glaring at the detective, the manager finally pulls off his bow tie and loosens his collar, his face flushed.

"Esmeralda's not crazy, guys. Just a little . . . touched."

"You mean loony tunes?" Jameson growls.

"I think the medical term is schizophrenic. And diabetic," Gigi argues. "Who wouldn't be, living on the streets? There's no telling what she eats." The young woman looks at Maxzyne. "This is one part of your crazy story that I do believe. I have a few of these paintings myself."

Ray looks at her in surprise. "You do?"

"Yeah. I like them. And her. She's a street artist, doing what she loves, and I admire her for it. I give her odds and ends from my art supply stash sometimes."

"What for?" Perplexed, Ray polishes the silver rims of his eyeglasses.

"Because I think she's brave, and selling her little paintings beats begging on the street. Lots of history's great artists painted for their suppers, you know."

Maxzyne clutches Faith, her voice trembling in relief. "Then you know I'm telling the truth, Gigi—we've got to save the mannequins."

"That's what you say. But I don't get the 'mannequins coming to life' thing. And don't forget—I own them. They're mine to use. But you've got my attention, kid."

"Well, that's a start!" Ray announces. "Look out,

folks, maybe Goth Girl has a heart after all!" Tossing her hair, Gigi shoots him a dirty look.

Mr. Tracy steps forward. "Yeah? Well, my heart only beats for the bottom line. Who's going to pay for all this damage?" He taps his foot impatiently. "Ruined clothes? Staff overtime? Why, it's going blow my weekly budget. I say it's a matter for the police. Sorry, kid, you've got to pay if you play."

Jameson stands at attention. "Want me to call it in, boss? Mr. Tracy gives a curt nod. "Sergeant Parker's on speed dial, sir." Jameson pushes the button on his phone.

"B-but there must be something else! I'll do anything, Mr. Tracy!"

"The last thing I need is a make-believing, runaway kid in my store! No, Missy, you've done enough damage!" The manager shakes his head. "And nobody breathes a word about this to the New York office—you hear me?" He glares at Jameson, Gigi, and Ray, who nod together. "They'd have my head—and if they do, I'll have yours." He points at the mannequins, chuckling. "No pun intended."

He turns back to Maxzyne. "So what else you got, kid? Your allowance?" He smirks. "Enough to pay for the goods, my pain and suffering, these ruined clothes? Sure, let's settle this the old-fashioned way."

"No. I don't have enough for all that, sir." Maxzyne

shakes her head, clutching Faith to her chest. "But maybe there's something else." Tears prick her eyes as she offers the doll to Mr. Tracy. "Here. She's all I have." Her voice is faint. "So if you'll please save the mannequins . . ."

Gigi snorts. All eyes turn to Mr. Tracy, who looks confused. "She thinks a doll's going to win *him* over?" Gigi whispers, wincing when Ray jabs her with an elbow.

Jameson waves his phone. "Sergeant Parker's on his way, sir . . . uh, sir?" The detective's mouth drops open in surprise as Mr. Tracy reaches down to accept Maxzyne's doll. Stroking the doll's round cheek with his fat thumb, he nods. "She's a Modern Heroine doll, right?"

Maxzyne nods, blinking back her tears as the others watch in amazement. "Her name's Faith, sir." She swallows hard. "Faith Livingston, the—"

"The famous American artist who quilts and paints her political beliefs, or some such thing. At least, according to my wife, Dolores."

Gigi laughs, clapping her hand over her own mouth. Ray gives her a warning look.

Maxzyne's eyes widen. "You know about Faith, Mr. Tracy? Wow, that's so cool. She's my favorite artist in the whole world! When I grow up, I want to be just like her."

Mr. Tracy stares at the doll, muttering to himself. "Faith? I gave up faith. First in ever having kids, lately in ever finding this doll for my wife. I called every Modern Heroine store and tried to back order it, but no luck. They stopped making it." Sighing, he looks at Maxzyne. "Faith is the only doll missing in my wife's collection—and she's got quite the collection, believe me." He pushes the doll back into the girl's hands. "Here. I can't take your doll, kid."

"But you have to take her, Mr. Tracy! It's only fair after all the trouble I caused. Maybe I can't save Elise, but I can do the right thing for once." She straightens the doll's braids and dress. A tear rolls down her chin, falling on Faith's cheek. Maxzyne wipes her eyes with the back of her hand, her bottom lip quivering. "You understand, don't you, Faith?" She holds the doll out.

Mr. Tracy looks uncomfortable, but accepts the doll once more.

In a flash, Maxzyne rushes to her tote bag. "Wait! I almost forgot! She has accessories— all kinds of stuff. See?" Unzipping a side pocket, she takes out a tiny canvas, brushes, paint set, palette, and quilted banner.

"Are you sure about this, kid?" The manager looks doubtful. "I know how collectors are with their dolls. Especially my Dolores—they're her adopted children."

Maxzyne pushes the small accessories into his hand and steps away. Hiding behind her braids for a moment, she gulps, blinking back her tears. "Then I know she's going to a good home, sir."

Mr. Tracy puts the little items in his pocket. "Well, okay, if you're really sure. I know my wife will be overjoyed to adopt her." And then, under the dark bristles of his mustache, Mr. Tracy smiles! He looks at the doll, his eyes crinkling with delight.

Maybe he has a kind heart after all, Maxzyne thinks. *Wow, he must really love his wife.*

"Thanks, kid. This'll sure make her Easter." He turns, still smiling, and gives a nod to Jameson. "You can call off the cops—we'll handle it in-house." He turns back, pointing his finger at Maxzyne. "And you need to help my staff *clean* house, young lady! Ray, be sure she helps get this place ship-shape."

"Will do, sir."

Mr. Tracy looks at her. "I should call your parents, kid."

Maxzyne hangs her head. "I promise to clean up the mess we—I mean, I made, sir. I know I learned my lesson."

The manager shakes his head. "I'm counting on that elbow grease, young lady!"

Disappointed, the detective eases the phone back into his pocket. "I still get credit for catching her, don't I, boss?"

Mr. Tracy rolls his eyes, waving him off. "We'll talk about it later." He holds the doll in the crook of his arm. "Right now, I have to find a big Easter basket with all the trimmings for Faith here . . . wait 'til Dolores sees her . . . this is really going to knock her socks off . . ." He grins at his employees.

Ray and Gigi are speechless. Jameson shrugs, pulling aside the heavy drape. Mr. Tracy exits, the doll nestled in the hollow of his arm. "Don't forget to unlock the employee entrance—the staff is free to leave now. Got that, Jameson?"

"Will do, boss!" The heavy curtain folds fall back into place behind them.

Suddenly, Gigi gasps, pointing at the window. "Look! Over there!"

20

C'est Miraculeux (It's a Miracle)

THE THREE TURN. They are shocked to see Peppin slowly shake himself from head to fuzzy tail. With a whimper and wag of his tail, he nudges Elise's frozen hand with his nose. Maxzyne's heart nearly bursts to see her blink, smile, and then lean over to stroke the dog. "*Bravo bon petit!* (Good boy!)" Straightening up, she looks at Maxzyne. Her eyes are filled with happiness. Then she races over to Aloin and Veronique to help them from their awkward positions.

"*Ma petite!* (My little one!) You are safe!" Aloin buries his face in Elise's blonde hair.

Veronique folds slender arms around both daughter and husband. "Ah, *cherie!*" Her voice breaks. "What has happened? Aloin, are we truly safe?" The elegant mannequin looks nervously in Gigi's direction.

Elise wriggles out from under her mother's arm. She runs to give Maxzyne a bear hug. Breaking apart, the girls trade fist bumps between little hops of joy. "It's okay, I think. I told them everything, Elise. Now it's up to Gigi." Maxzyne gives Gigi a winsome, hopeful smile.

Ray is first to speak. "Goth Girl, even you can't rain on this sunny parade, can you?" He shrugs, grinning. "There's got to be something else we can recycle for that sculpture of yours!"

"Yeah, I'd start with the Chromatones!" Maxzyne suggests, shuddering.

"The Chromatones!" Gigi and Ray look puzzled.

"What do you have against them?" Ray asks.

"Do tell, Maxzyne." Gigi raises one eyebrow. "Our window won an award last Halloween when we featured them. There's a special chip inside that makes them turn toward any movement. So whenever someone passed, they looked like they were trying to escape from the window."

Ray nods. "Yep, the crowds loved it!"

Gigi playfully elbows Ray. "My idea."

So that was it! Motion sensors. "No wonder those creeps were all over me!" Maxzyne exclaims. She throws her arm around Elise's neck. "Well, I'll take old mannequins any day!"

From the corner, Aloin politely clears his throat.

"Ahem . . . *excusez moi* (excuse me) . . . I don't think we've been properly introduced, *mademoiselle*." He strides over to Gigi. Then he confidently extends his hand. "*Mademoiselle* Gigi? Aloin. *Enchanté* (Pleased to meet you)."

Gigi is somewhat surprised. She slowly extends her hand, silver bangles clinking. Aloin raises her slim wrist to his mouth. He gives it a light kiss as he looks her in the eye. The dragon on her neck pulses again. It flushes pink. "Uh, pleased to meet you . . . Aloin. Gigi's just a nickname for Goth Girl. But you do make it sound so . . . charming, so French." Two bright red spots appear on her pale cheeks.

Not to be outdone, Veronique approaches Ray. She smiles timidly. "*Allo, je m'appelle* (Hello, my name is) Veronique." She gives Ray a quick air kiss on each cheek.

"Well, gee, I, uh . . . hello there!" Now it's Ray's turn to blush. "The name's Ray. Very nice to meet you, ma'am." He bows low.

Veronique squeezes his hand. "*Enchanté* . . . Ray."

Gigi steps away from Aloin. She looks perplexed. "Here's what I don't get. If you mannequins are real—and you do appear real, too real, I'd say— what's the catch? What happened to bring you back to life just now?"

Veronique reaches for Aloin's hand. "*Va, continue ta histoire* (Go on with your story). Maybe it will help, *cherie*."

With a worried glance, Aloin nods. "Perhaps it will, my dear." He squeezes her hand. "You see," Aloin begins hesitantly, "We were the last mannequins made by the Parisian Charm Mannequin Company in Milwaukee."

"Oh, really? I had no idea. Did you?" Ray looks at his assistant. She shrugs, shaking her head.

"See, I told you these mannequins were a piece of history," he scolds her.

"Allow me to explain." Ray, Gigi, and Maxzyne gather around Aloin, waiting. With one arm encircling Elise and the other holding his wife's hand, he begins. "Pierre Beaumont was the owner of the factory at the time of our manufacture. He was a very happy man. He had a loving wife, a beautiful, healthy daughter, a successful business. Overall, a very good life."

"*La vie en rose* (The good life)," Veronique echoes.

"The Beaumonts were rich and well regarded in the community. They took their social responsibilities very seriously, including the need to help others less fortunate. You know, the poor, the sick, and people with troubles of all kinds. They were known to be very *bienfaisant*, er, charitable. Especially Mrs. Beaumont. She often helped women and children through bad times."

"Like the homeless?" Gigi motions with her thumb to the street outside the window.

"Or kids without moms and dads?" Maxzyne offers, remembering Esmeralda's son.

"*Oui*. All of those things," Aloin nods.

Gigi taps her foot impatiently, hands on hips. "I still don't see what this has to do with—"

"*S'il vous plait* (Please). Allow me to continue."

"Patience, Gigi. It's not every day a mannequin tells a tale!" Ray reminds her.

Veronique raises a slender eyebrow. "And we do not know how long the *enchantement* (magic) will last. *Mon cher* (My dear), please. Talk faster!"

"As you wish, *cherie*. And so one cold January day, Monsieur Beaumont was at the factory. Madame and her *jeune fille* (daughter) brought food, warm socks, and gloves to the Women's Home and Work House. As they were climbing the steep, icy stairs, the young daughter slipped and had a terrible fall." Aloin's voice grows soft. "*Une catastrophe!* (A tragedy!)"

"You mean . . . did she die?" Maxzyne fusses nervously with a braid. She looks at Aloin and Veronique. They nod gloomily. Peppin gives a sad howl.

"And to make matters worse, the mother died soon after, of the winter sickness. It was common in that day and in those places."

"*Mal chance* (Bad luck), Papa!"

"*Oui*, Elise. Very bad luck. And so, on the day he buried his wife next to his daughter, Monsieur Beaumont returned to the factory. He paid all his workers double their wages and locked the doors behind them. Alone and overcome with grief, taking

neither meals nor sleep, he made a copy of his family from happier times." Aloin closes his arms protectively around Elise and Veronique. "We are that family."

"Ohhhhhh . . ." Maxzyne sighs. What a beautiful, sad story. "What happened to Mr. Beaumont?" she asks, thinking of her own father.

"Soon after we were made, Monsieur Beaumont died, also of the winter sickness. The factory was closed forever. We were the last mannequins. We were made and designed by a brokenhearted man. It was the talk of the town when we were sold at auction. Soon afterward we were on our way to Chicago."

"And the magic? What makes it happen?" Maxzyne wonders aloud.

"Oh, *oui, c'est miraculeux!* (Yes, it's like a miracle!)" Veronique beams at Maxzyne.

"The magic has only happened twice, child. Each time because of you." Aloin looks at her gratefully.

"Me? What did I do?"

"Perhaps because you give from the heart, *ma petite* (my little one). Your generosity is in the spirit of the Beaumont family." Veronique and Elise look at her, smiling.

"Really?" Maxzyne thinks hard for a few seconds. "Okay, Esmeralda said something about me giving money for her painting. But what about this time? What happened just now to make you real again?"

"You don't know?" Veronique shakes her head, amazed.

Elise rushes forward to give Maxzyne another hug. "It's because of Faith, Maxzyne! You gave up your doll for me! For us!" The mannequin family gathers around Maxzyne.

Ray gives her a pat on the back. "Saw it with my own eyes, missy!"

Gigi interrupts. Her voice is brisk. "So, how long do we have—you mannequins, I mean—until this 'generous spirit' wears off?"

"I know that look, Goth Girl," Ray teases. "Having second thoughts about them losing their heads?"

"Their heads are safe with me, Ray!" she retorts, tossing her hair. "Anyone with half a brain can see that these mannequins are special."

Aloin, Veronique, and Elise hug each other fiercely. Peppin yelps, his bedraggled tail thumping on the floor.

"And I think I know exactly where this mannequin family belongs."

"Oh, Gigi, where?" Elise looks worried. Maxzyne takes her hand.

"As long as we are together, Madame Gigi." Aloin smiles at his family.

Gigi nods, thinking out loud. "Ray, you know

those empty storefronts waiting to be rented around town? Especially here in the city Loop?"

"Sure, like the shopping center across the street. They've got window space in their mall overlooking Randolph Street right now. What're you thinking?"

"Well, you taught me a blank window's like an empty canvas, right?" He nods. "What if the mannequins were a part of Chicago's Pop Up Art Program? Instead of dark, empty windows, folks get a chance to see projects done by local artists. But in this case, why not with a historical twist? Use the vintage aspect. Imagine . . . Chicago, early twentieth century." Warming to the idea, she talks faster. "You know, there might even be grant money in this!"

Excited, Gigi smiles. Her long eyelashes flutter. Her almond eyes crinkle until they nearly disappear.

"Great idea, *Artiste*!" Ray claps her on the back. "Save these mannequins and make a name for yourself, too."

"Yay!" Still holding hands, Maxzyne and Elise jump with excitement. "Hear that, Elise?" Maxzyne shouts. "She's going to make you part of history!"

"*C'est bien* (That's good)," Aloin smiles at his wife. "Yes, a good idea, I think."

"Me? History, *mon cher*?" Veronique protests. "But I am not old! I am French!" She straightens up, head held high with indignant pride. Everyone laughs until even Veronique joins in.

Maxzyne turns to Gigi. She shyly tugs on her arm. "Gigi? Think maybe you could display some of Esmeralda's paintings, too? Maybe someone would see them and want to help her?"

The young woman nods in agreement. "Great idea, kid. And we could feature other artists in similar conditions. I've seen them out there on the sidewalks. Real starving artists."

"Sounds like you're going to be busy writing grant proposals, Goth Girl," Ray chuckles.

"That's me. Saving the world, one art exhibit at a time," she retorts good-naturedly.

Elise straightens her mother's shawl. "Maman, I need your help. I once promised Maxzyne I'd teach her some French. What do you suggest?"

"Oh, that is easy, *ma petite*." Veronique makes a grand sweep of the silk scarf around her neck. She gives Maxzyne a knowing look.

"There are only two words that a French lady must know."

"Really? Just two?" Maxzyne is unconvinced. "In the whole French language?"

"*Oui*, my dear." Veronique puts her hand on Maxzyne's shoulder. "Just two. The only two you need."

"So what are they?" Maxzyne looks at Elise, who only shrugs.

"*Bel esprit* (Wit), of course! Go on, repeat after me." Veronique closes her eyes, listening intently.

"*Bel esprit*?"

"*Oui*. Very nice." Veronique nods her approval. She claps lightly.

"But what does it mean?"

"What it means to be French, my dear." Maxzyne is confused. "Not just speaking French—*non*! One must have a fine mind, too." Aloin nods approvingly. Veronique continues. "You see? To be French, is to be a cultivated, highly intelligent person. To have true *bel esprit*."

"Like you, Maman?"

"*Oui, ma petite*. Like me, like you. And especially like our dear friend, Maxzyne."

Ray appears beside the two girls. He offers them an aerosol can and two white towels. "Ladies, we don't want to be here all night. Maxzyne, I want to see some elbow grease make those fingerprints disappear!"

Solemnly, the two girls head to the window, polishing cloths in hand. Maxzyne sprays "*Bel Esprit*" in foaming, white letters on the glass. The girls each take a corner, making their way to the middle, rubbing the glass 'til it squeaks.

Aloin steps forward. "How may we help, Ray?"

"Well, there's a ton of goods to be brought in so we can set up. It's all waiting just outside the curtain there." He turns, smiling at Veronique. "Ma'am, you look like a lady who loves working with real flowers as much as wearing them."

"But of course, Ray. *Comment puis-je aider*? (How can I help?)"

"Well, I'll need a hand with the blossoms out there. Could use some arranging, too."

With everyone's help, the window space is soon transformed into a sparkling showcase of elegant flower arrangements, colorful items for the home, unusual kitchen gadgets, and boxes of gourmet goodies. The old clocks hang from the ceiling. It gives the whole display a connection to history as well as a timely reminder of the Easter shopping deadline.

Maxzyne admires the display. "Wow, this is so cool. Maybe I want to be a—what's it called again, Gigi?"

"Visual display merchandiser. If Ray hasn't retired by the time you're old enough, he'll teach you everything retail, Maxzyne."

"I thought you were going to be an artist," Elise reminds her.

"Oh . . . yeah." Maxzyne considers. "Maybe I can do both. Like Gigi."

Hiding a smile, from high on the ladder, Gigi puts the finishing touches on the lighting. Outside the window, an old SUV pulls up, horn honking. "Oh, there's my friend, Mike!" She quickly jumps down. "He's here to help me with the mannequins. Er, I mean—you know, getting the family to my loft." She looks at Ray sheepishly. "Well, they'll need a place to stay, right?"

"Sounds like a plan to me." He waves through the window at Mike. "I'll help walk them out the employee entrance." In gentlemanly fashion, he offers Veronique his arm. Smiling, she hands him a bouquet she arranged from extra bits of ribbon and leftover roses. Aloin follows close behind, pulling down his shirtsleeves and buttoning his starched cuffs.

Maxzyne and Elise cling to each other.

"Elise! When will I see you again?" There is a bark from Peppin. Maxzyne kneels on the floor and gives him a hug. "Goodbye, boy." He whimpers and licks her cheek.

Elise's voice shakes. "I don't know . . . it sounds like we might be in a window around here. But whatever happens, you won't forget me, will you?"

"Forget you? Are you kidding? This has been the best, worst night of my life!"

"Me, too. The best ever." Elise gives

Maxzyne a fierce hug. The bell pendant tinkles merrily on the gold chain around Elise's slender neck.

"Maxzyne! Your necklace!"

"You know what, Elise?" Maxzyne smiles. She centers the clasp on the back of Elise's neck. "I want you to have it. That way, you'll always remember me, even if I'm not around to get us both into trouble."

"But it was a gift from your father! What will he say?"

"He'll say, 'It was a small trade for something bigger—friendship.' And anyway, you're more than a friend, you know. We're—"

"—sisters!" They shout, grinning.

"But I don't have anything to give *you*," Elise worries. She pulls her pockets apart. Outside, a horn honks impatiently. "There must be something," she frets. Her finger catches on the broken daisy trim. The loose threads give her an idea. Elise rips along the seam of daisies. She hands one to Maxzyne. "I know it's not much, but . . ."

"Follow the daisy and find a friend—or sister!" Maxzyne finishes the sentence for her. The two smile at each other. Outside, there is another impatient honk.

Gigi appears beside them. "Maxzyne, Elise has to go now! Mike's double-parked. Hurry, Elise."

Tearfully, the girls hug again. There is a final flurry of fist bumps. Then Elise disappears through the heavy curtain and is gone.

In the suddenly quiet space, Gigi hands Maxzyne her plastic tote bag. "Okay, time to get you back home where you belong. But first, let's not add shoplifting to the list of trouble. Jameson would be all over that! You've got your own clothes, right?"

Nodding, Maxzyne removes the red, suede ankle boots and denim jacket. Gigi holds up the nubby lavender robe and Maxzyne shimmies into the soft robe and ties the sash.

"No shoes?"

"Nope, my flip-flop broke on the way over here. See?" She pulls the broken sandal out of her bag.

"Well, here's your first lesson as an artist *or* a visual display merchandiser." Gigi pulls something orange and black, with a trailing cord, out of her basket. Plugging it into a nearby outlet, she waves it at Maxzyne. "An artist's go-to gadget—the glue gun!" She points the gun at Maxzyne's broken flip-flop, easily repairing the broken strap with warm wax. "Just give it a minute to cool, okay?"

Nodding, Maxzyne blows hard on the strap. Then she slides on the repaired sandal.

Outside, there is another honk and the flashing of lights. Aloin, Elise, and Veronique wave from the SUV before it turns on State Street. Maxzyne swallows hard, hearing Peppin's barking. There is a sudden crack of thunder.

A flash of lightning makes Gigi jump. "Drat! It's pouring," she says, frowning. "I was just going to walk you home. Look at that wind. Not even an umbrella will stop this rain. It's going sideways." They watch as water loudly beats against the glass.

"We don't have to go through that scary basement again, do we, Gigi?"

"No, there's another way. We'll go to Crowne's lower level and take the pedway. I think I can find the freight elevator for your building."

"Cool! Just keep me away from those Chromatones!"

"From what I saw, they're just as scared of you!" Laughing, Gigi picks up her work basket.

"Do you think if I paint them, they won't seem as scary?" Maxzyne looks at Gigi.

"Now you're thinking like an artist, Ms. Merriweather. Paint away!"

The two walk out of the window, letting the curtain fall into place behind them. Over by the Japanese maple tree, Maxzyne spots Ray leaning against his cart. He is talking to Ms. Mitchell. She watches him shyly offer the older woman Veronique's delicate rose bouquet. The elegant woman's cheeks turn pink and her eyes sparkle. Gigi skirts around the couple, but not before Maxzyne overhears Ray.

"Don't know about you, but I'm starved after all this overtime, Lady Mitchell. Any chance you'd like to join me for a bite to eat? There's this little place across the street. It serves a nice chicken pot pie . . ."

Ms. Mitchell beams. "Downtown Diner? Yes! And they have a lovely chicken salad. That and a pot of tea would be just perfect, wouldn't it?" Ray offers Ms. Mitchell his arm. The two wander off toward the employee exit.

"Mission accomplished," Gigi says under her breath, chuckling. She and Maxzyne stop at the bubbling fountain for a minute. Gigi props up the drooping forsythia one last time. Maxzyne can't help shrinking back into the leaves when Jameson appears.

"Got to watch that flower stuff," he warns Gigi. "Took forever to scrub it off, and I had to change shirts!"

Gigi nods, turning to look for Maxzyne. "Hey, that means you, too. You'll get pollen all over your robe." Maxzyne steps out of the leaves. She does not look at Jameson.

"You taking the kid back to her place now?" Maxzyne's stomach lurches. She wants to disappear inside her fluffy robe.

"Yep, that's where we're headed."

"Well, as long as you stay on the right side of the law, we won't have any trouble. Will we, Miss?"

Maxzyne nods. She is afraid if she looks at him, he might change his mind about those handcuffs. Without warning, he reaches down to shake her hand.

"Hey, thanks for giving up that doll. Mr. Tracy was in such a good mood he finally promoted me to full store detective. How 'bout that?"

Breaking into a grin, she salutes. "Congratulations, sir!"

Gigi rolls down her sleeves and picks up her workbasket. "That's enough for today. Let's go." She motions Maxzyne to follow her as she steps on the escalator heading down.

They reach the lower level. Maxzyne glances at the Lollipop & Soda Shop. She feels ashamed of the mess she made earlier. A mop and bucket of soapy water stand to one side of the glass counter. Gigi digs into her workbasket and hands her a pair of rubber gloves.

"We saved the floor for you, missy." Gigi sets her work basket on the counter and sits on the nearest stool. Seconds later, she is scrolling through her cell phone messages.

Maxzyne clumsily wrings out the mop and slowly wipes down the floor. "We really made a mess, didn't we?"

"You sure did, kid." Gigi gives her a sideways glance. "But not as much as I might have when I was your age." Her bracelets jangle as she points to the cupcakes, soda flavors, and candies. "All these color choices!"

"But I mixed too many flavors and colors," Maxzyne admits. "You know what that means?"

"Brown," they answer together.

Maxzyne wrings the mop one last time and rolls the bucket to the back of the counter. She hands the rubber gloves back to Gigi and together they leave the store. Maxzyne recognizes the deserted underground walkway that links the two buildings.

"I bet you'll make a good artist someday, Ms. Merriweather," Gigi chuckles. "Who knows? Maybe your artistic medium will be food."

"You really think I can be an artist, Gigi? Even if I'm always messing up?"

"Art thrives on mess. Just not in our store!" Maxzyne is thrilled that Gigi talks to her as if she were grown up. She stands taller, feeling older than ten. Almost as if they were equals. "A little organized chaos never hurt anyone," Gigi continues. "Creativity is like a thunderstorm in your head, right?" She waves her arms dramatically. "Crash! Boom!"

"Yeah, my mother says my head's in the clouds. That's what gets me in trouble."

"And that's how you'll make great art someday. A generous spirit, rich imagination, good at making a mess. Oh, and a whole lot of nerve." Gigi raises an eyebrow at Maxzyne. "You've definitely got nerve, Maxzyne." Pausing, she turns right at a large column in the middle of the pedway. Tucked into a corner, on the other side of the passageway, Esmeralda sits on the floor beside her battered suitcase.

"Hey, look! There's Esmeralda!" Gigi and Maxzyne walk toward the homeless woman. They step around her damp red cloak drying on the floor. Esmeralda is humming off-key. She looks up from her sketch pad.

"Staying dry down here, Esmeralda?" Gigi asks. The woman nods. She gives a half wave to Maxzyne.

"Going home, child?"

Maxzyne nods. "I hope I'll still see you around sometimes, Esmeralda."

"Oh, Esmeralda's never far. She'll always be where she supposed to be." Nodding, the woman returns to her sketch, humming as she draws.

Maxzyne and Gigi continue walking down the pedway. They turn right behind the next large column. Gigi points at an exit sign above the painted brown door. "This is you."

Stepping inside, she turns right again. Maxzyne follows her through another brown door. Ahead are the steel doors of the freight elevator for Maxzyne's building. Gigi pushes the button, waiting. Maxzyne's heart pounds, hearing the clanking gears of the elevator making its way toward them. "Seems to be working okay, now," Gigi declares. "But if you want, I can go with you."

"This is nothing." Maxzyne shrugs. "My parents are going to kill me when I get home."

"Anything I can do to help, Drama Queen?"

Maxzyne looks at Gigi's dragon tattoo, multicolored hair, and sky-high boots. She imagines her mother's reaction to them. *It was nice of Gigi to offer,* she thinks. But this is something she has to do herself. Growing up means taking responsibility.

"Um, no. But thanks, anyway. I guess I can handle it from here." The steel elevator door groans open, exposing the cold, gray interior. Maxzyne steps in. "Bye, now. And tell Elise I'll look for her in the windows!" she calls. She waves as the door groans closed.

Alone again in the dreaded elevator, Maxzyne can't help chewing a braid as she pushes the button for the twenty-first floor. "Hey, Mr. Elevator. Don't even think about scaring me again."

With a whirring and grinding noise, the elevator car shoots upward. It makes her stomach lurch and her ears pop. Pinching her nose, she swallows, trying to adjust the pressure in her ears. Growing dizzy, she squints at the panel of buttons, trying to read the numbers. Seconds later, everything blurs as her vision fades in and out. Reaching for the rail, Maxzyne slides to the floor.

21

Better than La-La Land

"MAXZYNE! MAXZYNE! Can you hear me?" From far away, she hears the familiar voices call her name. Her parents' voices!

"D-Dad?" she answers weakly. She opens her eyes, but there is only darkness and the cold metal floor beneath her. "Mother?" The banging and pounding makes her head hurt, but at last the doors slide open. Cool air. She tries to stand up.

"Maxzyne!"

"Mother?" Lifting her head toward the familiar voice, Maxzyne feels heavy and drowsy.

"Jeffrey, can you please hold that door open? Max will carry her home."

"Sure, Mrs. Merriweather," answers the condo building doorman. "Good thing I noticed her on the closed circuit TV. Here, let me use this key." A dull, buzzing noise sounds. "That elevator repairman will be here soon. Better get this thing fixed before someone else gets stuck in here!"

"Well, we won't make too much of a fuss, since she did wander off by herself." Maxzyne feels a vague sense of guilt but can't quite remember what she might have done.

"Thanks, Jeffrey. I've got her now," a voice rumbles in her ear.

Strong arms reach out and cradle her gently. "Dad?" She looks up into her father's concerned face. "You're home!" She snuggles closer to his chest.

"Better than that, my little mermaid—*you're* home." He squeezes her even more tightly.

She has a vague recollection of mermaids, a planned rescue, and a trip to the pool by herself until . . . uh oh. It's all coming back to her now. *Breathe.* Dreamily, she inhales the warm smell of her father, a faint mix of soap, aftershave, and his favorite mints. One of her sandals drops to the floor.

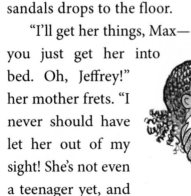

"I'll get her things, Max— you just get her into bed. Oh, Jeffrey!" her mother frets. "I never should have let her out of my sight! She's not even a teenager yet, and

I'm already having to worry . . ."

"Kids always want to stretch their wings, Mrs. Merriweather. But she didn't get far."

"Oh, yes, I did! I had the best adventure ever!" Maxzyne wriggles in her father's arms, trying to see past his shoulder. "Gigi had a dragon around her neck but turned out to be nice, the mannequins have a new home, I had a French lesson, and Mr. Tracy isn't mad anymore. And best of all, I have a sister— her name's Elise."

"Max? Should we call a doctor?" Mother's voice rises with worry.

"It's just a little bump, Geri. We'll see how she feels in the morning. You know our girl—always in La-La Land. Right, kiddo?"

Maxzyne nods, squeezing her father's arm. A cloth daisy falls through her fingers, fluttering to the floor. "Wait a sec! Stop a minute, Dad! Mother! Please, can you get that?" She points down at the carpeted floor, hoping to spot the daisy in the swirling green pattern. "Elise gave it to me!"

Mother bends down and plucks the daisy from the rug. "This? What in the world . . . and who is Elise?" Shaking her head, she hands the small flower to her daughter.

"Thanks!" Maxzyne clutches the dainty flower tightly in her hand and then relaxes back against her father's neck. A second later, she pops up, her braids brushing his cheek. "In Florida, can we play some computer games and look for sand dollars on the beach?"

"As long as we can snorkel, sail, play putt-putt, Frisbee, and cruise the boardwalk together. But I'm leaving my computer at home." He hugs her tight and gives her a wink. "Figure I'll spend some quality time with my girls."

They enter sideways through the familiar door. *Dad's being so gentle, not letting me bump against anything,* she thinks. How nice to feel warm and loved and to be home! Seeing the condo with its foyer mirror, the red silk carpet, and the gleaming hardwood floor, she knows that everyday things have never seemed so beautiful.

"Yes! And how about a swimming race, Dad? I know I'm faster than last year!" Maxzyne jerks upright, nearly bumping her head on his chin.

"You're on, mermaid. And I'll even talk your mom into letting us have corndogs, pizza, and hot fudge sundaes. How about that?"

"That's better than La-La Land, Dad! And maybe I'll paint them, too! Who knows, maybe I'll be a famous food artist." She smiles wide as he lowers her gently onto the familiar green comforter.

He strokes her cheek, nodding. "How about I make you a smoothie?"

"Raspberry?"

"You got it!" Father and daughter trade fist bumps as Maxzyne's mother enters the bedroom. She places the tote bag on the dresser.

"I'll pack your suitcase first thing tomorrow. But are you sure you're feeling okay?" With motherly concern, she sits on the bed near Maxzyne, one cool hand resting on her daughter's forehead.

"I'm fine. Promise. But I'm sorry I ran off without telling you. I just wanted to try out my new suit and—"

"—and I let my migraine get in the way, I suppose. I took my medicine and just fell sound asleep. When your father came home, he went to check on you, but you were gone! And it was so late. We were beside ourselves with worry!" Maxzyne squeezes her mother's hand, feeling terrible when her mother's eyes fill with tears.

"I'm just so glad you're safe." She strokes her daughter's braids. From the kitchen, the blender whirs, mixing ice, yogurt, and berries

"Does this mean I'm grounded for life?" Maxzyne asks timidly.

Her mother sniffs, unable to stop a small chuckle. "You're growing up so fast, young lady. But I still worry about you."

"I know. But I'll try not to make you worry so much from now on."

"Oh? And how is that going to happen?" The anxious tone creeps back into her voice.

"Lots more family time. You, me, and Dad doing fun things together. Besides . . ."

"Besides what?"

Maxzyne sits up in bed. "In just four more months, I'm eleven! That's practically grown up!" She falls back against the pillow, grinning. "Think of all the new stuff I'll want to do! But don't worry. I promise I'll always ask first before I—"

"One adventure at a time, Maxzyne." Her mother draws the covers up over her shoulders, turning to reach for the heart-shaped, satin pillow near the foot of the bed. Puzzled, she looks around the bedroom. "Honey?"

"Hmmmm?"

"Where's your doll? I don't see Faith."

"Oh, Mother. I'm kind of old for dolls, don't you think?" Snuggling deeper under the covers, Maxzyne yawns, sighs softly, and closes her eyes.

Discussion Guide

1. *Immediately, Mother's nose begins to twitch. Her lips purse tightly in annoyance. She grabs her daughter by the coat collar and begins to back away. But before Mother can get far enough, the homeless woman pulls a small painting from her bag. She pushes it into Maxzyne's hand. Mother strides off, dragging her daughter along.*

   - Tell what the word "annoyance" means to you.

   - Tell why Mother might be annoyed by the homeless woman.

   - What does the action of pulling Maxzyne away from the woman say about Mother's character?

   - Explain why the homeless woman gave Maxzyne the small painting. Tell why she specifically chose to give it to Maxzyne.

   - Who is Maxzyne? What kind of a girl is she?

2. *Maxzyne tucks the doll, tiny easel, painting board, and paintbrush in her tote. Then she*

makes a final sweep of the room. She scoops a delicate necklace from the dresser, dropping it into a pocket inside the bag. At the last minute, she adds the homeless woman's painting. She carefully rolls it into the bag next to her doll.

- Maxzyne is packing her tote in preparation to go on an adventure. Explain why she packed the following items:

    - The doll – what is the significance of Faith, the Modern Heroine doll? Why is it important to Maxzyne?

    - The art supplies – why are they important to Maxzyne?

    - The necklace – tell the story behind the necklace.

    - Explain why she handles the homeless woman's painting with such care.

- If you were about to go on an adventure, much like Maxzyne's, which of your belongings would you take with you and why?

3. *"It would be a game if it wasn't so real!" Elise nervously smoothes her blonde ponytail and adjusts the daisy headband. "But I do like being a model more than being a mannequin. Even more, I love being a real girl. You're so lucky, Maxzyne!"*

- Tell why Maxzyne is lucky in Elise's eyes.

- Is Maxzyne lucky in your eyes? How so?

- Explain the difference of being a model as compared to being a mannequin.

- Explain the consequences if Maxzyne and Elise are not successful in their quest. Tell what is at stake for Maxzyne if she is not able to help the mannequin family.

4. *"Your goose is cooked, girls. Caught red-handed," accuses a booming, male voice.*

- Do you think that there were times when Maxzyne's wild imagination caused her to lose focus regarding their quest? Explain your answer.

- Do you think that Maxzyne's spontaneous love of fun and adventure served her well throughout the story? How so?

- Do you think that Maxzyne's lively nature helped Elise in any way? If so, tell how and why.

5. *Maxzyne's heart pounds. Where are they going? This whole contraption, this so-called dumbwaiter, seems rickety and dangerous. But if she can focus on pulling as steadily as possible, maybe she can stay calm. Breathe.*

- Elise is assuming the leadership role
  in this scene. Explain why.

- Explain why Maxzyne has trouble focusing.

- Describe the danger involved in using
  the dumbwaiter. Is their friendship
  worth the risk? How so?

6. *Unable to stay silent, Maxzyne steps forward,
   waving her arms. "Hey! It's wasn't her fault,
   people! You can't blame her. It was me!"*

- Maxzyne's nature is beginning to change.
  Tell how she is starting to assume
  responsibility for her actions.

- What events caused her to cease thinking of
  herself and to begin thinking of others?

- Describe Maxzyne's relationship with Elise. Tell
  how it has changed over the course of the story.

7. *Struggling for answers, she runs back to Aloin.
   His loose collar gives him a sloppy look that he
   would not want anyone to see. Gently, Maxzyne
   reaches to button it. But when her fingers touch
   his smooth, cold skin, she backs away in horror.
   She nearly topples him. Even as he wobbles, he still
   looks as though he's disappointed in her. Maxzyne
   runs to Elise. "Elise! How do I help Esmeralda and
   get you back again? Somebody? Tell me!"*

- What does the act of gently buttoning Aloin's collar reveal about Maxzyne's changed character?

- Would the original Maxzyne even care or notice that Aloin desires to be dressed neatly at all times? How so?

- Tell why Aloin is disappointed in her.

- Explain how Maxzyne shares in the responsibility of the mannequins returning to their frozen state.

- Explain how Maxzyne is demonstrating compassion for Esmeralda.

- Tell of ways that her adventure with the mannequins has helped Maxzyne to develop a sense of compassion for others.

8. *"You learned to share. Out here on the street, don't see so much sharing going on." Esmeralda rises, hands on hips, surveying the evening street. "Nope. Thing is, I didn't know I'd be needing people to share when I left home just a girl." She sits slowly down on the suitcase, her high forehead wrinkling as she remembers.*

- Tell of ways that Maxzyne has learned to share throughout the course of the story.

- Explain why Esmeralda has chosen to share her story and artwork with Maxzyne. Could there be a special connection of some sort between the two? How so?

- Later in the story, Gigi mentions that she knows of Esmeralda's illnesses and also that Esmeralda has shared her artwork with her, as well. Could it be that there is a special quality within Gigi and Maxzyne that only Esmeralda is aware of? If so, explain what this special quality might be.

- Do you think Esmeralda was misunderstood as a child, much like Maxzyne is? Could it be their artistic nature that causes them to be misunderstood? How so?

9. *"You know what, Elise?" Maxzyne smiles. She centers the clasp on the back of Elise's neck. "I want you to have it. That way, you'll always remember me, even if I'm not around to get us both into trouble."*

- Tell how the act of giving Elise the necklace shows Maxzyne's growth as a character.

- Why was giving away Faith, the Modern Heroine doll, important to Maxzyne?

- In what ways did Maxzyne learn about the true meaning of generosity and of friendship?

- Tell how her bravery was tested.

- Was Maxzyne's loyalty tested
  in this story? How so?

- Explain how she came to better understand
  the values of kindness and compassion.

- How about you? As a result of reading this
  story, what have you learned regarding the acts
  of loyalty, bravery, generosity, and friendship?

Book Discussion Guide created by

www.debbiegonzales.com

About the Author and Illustrator

Photo by Beate Hill

Author Caroline Lee enjoys living in the city of Chicago with her husband Rebel. When she's not writing, she can sometimes be found walking along Lake Michigan. She loves cupcakes, brussels sprouts, and texting her niece, Rebecca. Don't tell anybody, but she's also a teeny bit scared of riding the freight elevator in her building.

www.Maxzyne.com

Illustrator Jonathan Wolfe lives in Seattle, Washington with his hedgehog Trevor, where he spends his days drawing and drinking too much coffee.

www.Bellwolfe.com

CPSIA information can be obtained
at www.ICGtesting.com
Printed in the USA
FFOW05n2225210415